Mighty-One
the
Wizard
and
Other Stories

by
ENID BLYTON

Illustrated by
Maggie Downer

AWARD PUBLICATIONS LIMITED

JF

For further information on Enid Blyton please contact
www.blyton.com

ISBN 1-84135-214-4

This compilation text copyright © 2003 The Enid Blyton Company
Illustrations copyright © 2003 Award Publications Limited

Enid Blyton's signature is a trademark of
The Enid Blyton Company

This edition entitled *Mighty-One the Wizard and Other Stories*
published by permission of The Enid Blyton Company

This edition first published 2003
3rd impression 2004

Published by Award Publications Limited,
27 Longford Street, London NW1 3DZ

Printed in Singapore

CONTENTS

Mighty-One the Wizard

There once lived a golden-haired princess whose name was Mirabelle. She was sweet and good, and the King and Queen were proud of her. But one day she vanished from the palace, and for two whole months not a word was heard of her.

Then the North Wind, who blows into every hole and corner at some time or other, came with a message to the King.

"I have seen the Princess Mirabelle," he said, in his blustery voice, and he blew all round the palace, making the King and Queen shiver in their shoes.

"Where is she, oh where is she?" cried the King.

"She is imprisoned in the castle of Mighty-One, the wizard of Ho-Ho Land," answered the wind, blowing the King's crown to one side. "I saw her at the top window, and I touched her pretty golden hair and knew that she was Mirabelle. You must send a message to the wizard if you want her back."

"Oh, thank you for telling me," said the King. The wind bowed and flew off, setting all the curtains swaying in the wind, and blowing over a big vase of flowers.

The King called a meeting and all the nobles came to it. They discussed what must be done to rescue the poor princess, but nobody dared to offer to go to the wizard's castle. So at last the King called the North Wind back again, and told him to go to Ho-Ho Land and ask the wizard what they must do to get Princess Mirabelle back.

The wind was quite willing. He was afraid of nothing and nobody. He swept off, sending a trail of dust down the road, making everyone there sneeze and cough.

In two days the North Wind blew back again. He had been to Ho-Ho Land in a

gale of a hundred miles an hour, and had spoken with the wizard Mighty-One.

"He says, O King, that you and all your court must journey to his castle. He will allow you to take Mirabelle back with you on condition that you are able to do three things." The wind blew round the palace room, and the King drew his cloak closely round him. This North Wind was really a rough fellow.

"What are the three things?" asked the King eagerly. "I am rich and I can buy anything in the world!"

"First you must give the wizard something that nobody in the world has set eyes on before," said the North Wind. "Second, you must ask the wizard to do something he is not able to do – and I'm sure I don't know what you'll think of for that, because, O King, by his magic powers he can do almost anything in the world! And third, you must tell him what he is thinking of at the moment you stand before him!"

The King turned pale. How could he do three such difficult things? They were impossible! He might perhaps get some treasure out of the depths of the earth, a precious stone that no one had set eyes on before – but how could it be got without being seen? As for asking the wizard to do something that he couldn't do, well, that was certainly a puzzle. Thirdly, how in the world was he to know what the wizard was thinking of when he saw him? The King groaned aloud.

"Suppose I fail?" he said to the wind. "What will happen?"

"Oh, you and all your court will

become Mighty-One's servants," the wind answered, puffing into the King's ear.

"In that case, I and my court will certainly not go," said the King, decidedly. "I shall not become any wizard's servant."

But the Queen thought differently. She wanted the Princess Mirabelle back again, even if it meant that all of the court, herself and the King too, fell into the wizard's power.

"Even if we do have to become his servants, we shall at least be where Mirabelle is," she said. "We must

certainly go. But first we must think what to take with us than no one has ever set eyes on before."

The King and Queen and all the court tried in vain to think of something. The best idea they could get was to send a blind dwarf underground and bid him to search about until he found a ruby.

"As he is blind he won't see it," said the King. "He shall put it into a casket as soon as he finds it, and no one shall open the casket until we stand before the wizard himself."

"But how will the dwarf know whether the stone is a ruby or not?" asked the Queen. "If he is blind he won't be able to tell."

"Oh, don't make difficulties," said the King, snappily. "I'm doing my best."

"But if the wizard opens the casket and sees a bit of coal there instead of a precious stone, he will be very angry," said the Queen. "And how will you know what his thoughts are?"

"Oh, I'll think of those things on the journey," said the King. "It will take us six days, so there will be plenty of time to think."

He sent the blind dwarf under the earth with a casket. Presently the little creature came back and gave the casket to the King. It rattled when he shook it and the King hoped that there was a beautiful ruby inside. He did not dare look, of course, for then somebody would have seen it.

He and the Queen set off to Ho-Ho Land with all their court. There were a hundred and two travellers, some in coaches and some on horseback. They travelled slowly, for some of the roads were not good. On the way the King tried to think of something he could ask the wizard to do which would be impossible. But he couldn't think of anything at all!

At last they all arrived in Ho-Ho Land. It was a strange country, with the sky very low so that it seemed more like a high ceiling than a sky. Far away on a mountain-top could be seen the wizard's magnificent castle, shining brightly, for it was made of gold mixed with blue glass.

The court halted at the foot of the mountain. It was drawing near night-time, too late to visit the wizard that day. The servants quickly put up the tents that the court had used for the last five nights, and prepared a meal. The King and Queen dined with their nobles, and nobody dared say a word to the King, for he had been quite unable to think of how to fulfil the second and third

conditions of the wizard, and was looking very worried indeed.

He was so worried that he could not sleep that night. When dawn came he got up and slipped out of his tent. The sun was not yet risen, but the eastern sky was full of gold. He wandered up the hillside, gazing at the shining castle above him, trying in vain to think of something he could ask the wizard to do, which he would be unable to.

He sat down on a big stone, put his head into his hands and groaned loudly. He hadn't sat there for more than five minutes when he felt something licking his hand. He looked up and saw a fine sheepdog looking at him, with a very

thick, curly coat. Just behind him was a bright-eyed shepherd lad with a crook.

"What ails you, master?" asked the shepherd, kindly. "I and my dog, Curly, heard you groaning and sighing."

"Ah, shepherd, you can do nothing to help me," said the King. "I and all my men whom you see down there will be servants of Wizard Mighty-One before nightfall!"

"Well, why do you not run away?" asked the shepherd lad, in astonishment. "There is plenty of time."

"Alas! I cannot run away, because I have come to try to rescue my daughter, the Princess Mirabelle," said the King. "The wizard keeps her imprisoned in his castle. He will only let her go on three conditions – one, that I give him something no one else has ever seen – two, that I ask him to do a task he cannot do – three, that I tell him what his thoughts are when I am before him. The first condition I might manage, though it is hard enough, but the other two are too difficult for me."

The shepherd laughed.

"They seem to me to be easy," he said. "I could do them all – of that I'm sure!"

The King stared at him in astonishment. "Well, do them!" he said at last. "Do them, shepherd, and maybe you shall have my beautiful daughter to be your wife!"

"Done!" said the shepherd. "I have seen the lovely princess looking out of her tower window many a time this last month, and I would do anything in the world for her. But listen, O King – will you permit me to wear your tunic, cloak and crown, and pretend to be you today? For only if I do that can I outwit the wizard."

"Anything you like!" cried the King. "I will go and tell my courtiers now."

Off he went, the shepherd following nimbly, the curly-haired sheepdog gambolling after. In a few words the King told his nobles what was going to happen. They agreed to follow the shepherd that day, and to pretend that he was the King himself.

"But, woe betide him if he does not do all he says!" said the oldest courtier, feeling his sword. "For I will slay him if he has deceived you, O King!"

The King stripped off his silver tunic and took off his cloak of gold. He handed them to the shepherd who put them on. Then he took the King's glittering crown and placed that on his curly locks. A fine king he made, there was no mistake about that!

The King donned a suit belonging to one of his courtiers, and mixed with

them. Then up the hill the shepherd went, leading the way to the towering castle of glass and gold. He picked something from a bush on his way and put it into his pocket. The King could not see what it was. The shepherd hummed a jolly tune as he went, and the King felt lighter of heart than he had been for months!

At last they stood before the great wooden door of the castle. The big nails that studded the door were of shining gold. The shepherd knocked loudly.

The door swung open and the shepherd led the way in. The King and the courtiers looked round them in a scared manner as the great door swung to. They all wondered the same thing. Would they ever go out of that door – or would they have to stay inside as the wizard's servants for ever and ever?

The shepherd made his way into a room whose ceiling was so high that it seemed to be the sky. It was held up by tall slender pillars, and from the top to the bottom of these pillars burned green

tongues of flame. At the end of the great room sat Wizard Mighty-One, giant-like in form, and with eyes that shone like pieces of glowing ember.

"So you have come!" he said to the shepherd, thinking he was the King. "You think you can take your daughter from me by your cleverness? O King, you are very foolish. You and your nobles will be my servants, and the Princess Mirabelle will stay here all her life."

"Not so!" said the shepherd, with a laugh. "If I pit my wits against yours, O Mighty-One, I shall defeat you! Mirabelle shall leave this castle with me today!"

Mighty-One frowned and the flames that burned all the way up the pillars turned from green to red.

"You have three conditions to fulfil," he said sharply. "What was the first?"

"The first, O Wizard, was that I should bring to you something that no one else in the world has ever set eyes on before," said the shepherd, bowing.

"Ho!" said the wizard, mockingly. "And what have you brought me? Some precious stone from under the earth? Some marvel from beneath the seas? None will be of use, for at some time or another worms or beetles see everything under the ground, and fishes swim around everything in the sea."

"Nay, I bring you something that no man, bird, animal or insect has ever seen," said the shepherd. He put his hand into his tunic pocket and brought out a brown hazel-nut!

"Open this shell, Mighty-One," he said, "and inside you will see a close-hidden nut, seen by no eyes but yours before."

He placed the nut in the long-fingered hand of the suprised wizard. Mighty-One frowned again and the flames, climbing the pillars, changed from red to purple. It was enough to make anyone shake with fear.

But the shepherd did not care. He smiled impudently at the angry wizard, and offered to crack the nut for him.

"Enough!" said the wizard, angrily. "I will not crack the nut. There is no need. I will accept the first condition, as

21

fulfilled. You have brought me something that certainly no eyes have seen before – the kernel of this nut. Now what was the second condition?"

"The second condition, O Mighty-One, was that I should ask you to do something you could not do," said the shepherd, his bright eyes twinkling.

"Ho!" said Mighty-One, pleased. "That is impossible!"

The shepherd turned and whistled low. His sheepdog, Curly, ran up to him. The shepherd plucked a long, curling hair from his coat.

He gave it to the wizard.

"Straighten this hair for me," he said.

The wizard looked at the shepherd as if he were mad. He took the hair and pulled it straight but it immediately shot back into curl again. He flattened it under his hand – it went back curly again. He took an iron from the air by magic and slowly ironed the curly hair up and down – but the more he ironed it, the curlier it became!

Then in a rage he wetted his finger and damped that curly hair – but as soon as it dried it sprang back into a tighter curl than ever!

He called magic to his help and muttered strings of enchanted words. The hair gradually became straight – but as soon as the wizard stopped muttering the words the hair curled again so tightly that there was no straightening it all!

The wizard threw down the hair in a rage and stamped his foot! The flames round the pillars shot up higher than ever and turned to orange, so that all the courtiers and the King trembled where they stood. Only the shepherd, grand in his cloak of gold and his bright crown, stood unafraid, smiling broadly.

"The second condition is fulfilled," said the wizard at last, in a furious voice. "You are cleverer that I thought you, O King. What was the third condition?"

"That I should tell you what you are thinking, O Mighty-One," said the shepherd.

"That is impossible," said the wizard, looking triumphantly at the shepherd. "No one can tell me what I am thinking."

The shepherd laughed loudly. His sides shook and his laugh echoed all round the great room. The King, hidden among his courtiers, wondered what there was to laugh at. He had watched the shepherd in wondering surprise when he fulfilled first one and then two of the wizard's conditions – but he did not see how the shepherd was going to defeat the wizard for the third time.

"Why do you laugh?" asked the wizard, angrily. "You will not be so merry when you find yourself and all your men my servants, prisoners in my castle! Why do you laugh, I say?"

"I laugh because I know your thoughts!" said the shepherd. "I know what you think, O Mighty-One! Your thoughts are easy to read!"

"What am I thinking then?" cried the wizard in a rage.

"O Wizard, you are thinking that I am the King!" cried the shepherd. "But I am not! I am only Strong-Arm, the shepherd!"

He pulled off his cloak and tunic and stood there in his rough jersey and thick hose, laughing at the astonished wizard.

"Tell truly!" he cried. "You were

thinking I was the King! Ah, I have read your thoughts, you see, Mighty-One! The third condition is fulfilled!"

The wizard saw that he was defeated. He gave a great howl and leaped up from his seat. There came a noise of thunder and the flames round the tall pillars roared like a fire. The castle shook and shivered and suddenly broke into a thousand pieces that flew away into the air, taking the wizard with them. Nothing was left at all, except only the seat on which the wizard had sat.

The King, the shepherd and the courtiers were thrown to the ground. They leaped up at once and watched the castle and the wizard vanishing in the distance. Then the King remembered his daughter, the Princess Mirabelle.

"She has been spirited away, too!" he cried – but she hadn't. She suddenly appeared nearby and ran to the King in delight, hugging and kissing him.

"Oh, Father, I am free at last!" she cried. Then she curtsied to the shepherd and thanked him for all he had done for

her, for, without him knowing it, she had heard everything from a nearby room.

Then, gladly and merrily, the King and Queen, the shepherd, the Princess and the courtiers set off home again. How glad they were to see the last of the lowering skies of Ho-Ho Land! Their people welcomed them home in delight, for they had been certain that they would never again see either the King or his daughter.

Princess Mirabelle fell in love with the bright-eyed shepherd long before she reached home, and in a short time they were married. Every bell in the land rang out on their wedding-day, and so loud was the noise that the Wizard Mighty-One, brooding in a faraway land, heard the joyful sound and frowned fiercely.

But he could do them no harm. He had been conquered by the sharp wits of a shepherd lad, and never again would he show his face to friend or foe.

A Very
Good Idea

Mr Nimble took off his big glasses and put them down beside him with a sigh.

"I've finished," he said. "See, doesn't the necklace look lovely?"

He held it up for his wife and three children to see. It certainly did look beautiful – and no wonder, because it belonged to the Queen herself! The necklace had been broken and some of the lovely beads had been lost.

So she had sent it to Mr Nimble, who was famous for making the most beautiful jewellery that could be bought in or out of Fairyland. His long, nimble fingers could thread the very smallest beads.

"I hope the goblins who live under-ground near us haven't heard about our mending the Queen's necklace," said his wife. "I'm sure if they had they would try and get it from us as we take it to the palace."

Well, the goblins had heard about it, and they certainly meant to get it from Mr Nimble when he set off to the palace with it. They had already made their plans.

Mr Nimble didn't know that a small goblin peeped in at his window each evening to see if the necklace was mended yet. He didn't know that a little

mouse listened to all he said and then ran off under the ground to tell the goblins. He didn't know that the goblins were preparing to lie in wait for him as he went on his way to the palace.

So he wasn't a bit worried. All the same, he and his wife thought it would be a good idea to set off to the palace at night, when it was dark. Their three children wanted to come, too.

"Very well," said Mr Nimble. "You shall come as well, and keep your eyes and ears open in case you hear any of those mischievous goblins."

So one dark night the whole family set out. But the little mouse heard their plan and had run to tell the goblins. They were all waiting in the woods for Mr Nimble and his little family.

"Now, not a sound!" said the head goblin. "Not a word! You, Jinky, can tackle Mr Nimble with me, and run off with the necklace as soon as you can get it. You, Smudge, can pin Mrs Nimble's hands behind her and tie a hanky over her mouth, because she can scream very loudly. And you three goblins can catch the children and spank them very hard if they yell."

"Right," said the goblins, and their green eyes gleamed. What a lot of money they would make when they sold the Queen's necklace! Witch Sharp-Eyes would buy it, they knew that.

Now, just as the Nimble family were setting foot in the wood, one of the sharp-eared children heard something. It was a sneeze!

A sneeze – in the wood! Someone must be hiding there. Perhaps it was the goblins. "I heard a sneeze," whispered the small boy, moving his long ears around like a rabbit. "Quick, we must go back home. The goblins are hiding in the wood!"

"I can smell them," said another of the children, and she twitched her woffly nose like a mouse.

"We can't go back. The goblins are surrounding us. I can hear them," said Mr Nimble, his pointed ears trembling as the little rustling sounds came to him.

"Oh, what shall we do? We shall be robbed of the beautiful necklace."

"Father Nimble – I know what we'll do," said Mrs Nimble suddenly. "There's a ditch near here and nettles grow in it – fierce stinging-nettles, with poison in the hairs on their leaves. Let's creep over to the ditch and pick some of them. Then we'll hold them in front of us, and what a shock the goblins will get when they feel the sting of the nettles!"

"Yes. They don't know anything about plants," said one of the children. "They're underground folk. They won't be able to understand it. Let's hiss like snakes as we go, and then when the goblins get stung by the nettles in the darkness they will think snakes have harmed them!"

The other children giggled. They thought this was great fun. None of them liked the goblins, who had often caught them and spanked them for nothing at all.

They crept to the ditch. They bent down low and crept beneath the nettles, for they were very, very small people. Mr Nimble took out his knife, and in a second he had cut down five nettles. Then he ran his knife a little way up each stalk to clear away any hairs or leaves that might sting his little family.

"Here you are," he said. "There's one each. Now keep together in a close bunch, and spread out the nettles all round us. Ready?"

"Sssssss!" answered the children, pretending to be snakes already. They moved forward, keeping close together, hissing loudly.

The goblins were puzzled. They wonderd what the hissing noise was. Ah, now they could hear the footsteps of the Nimble family. Good!

"Off we go!" cried the head goblin, and the little company swept down upon the Nimbles. But as soon as they reached them they touched the nettles.

Oooooh! How they were stung! How they smarted! What was it? What could it be? The Nimbles were there because the goblins could hear their footsteps – but who was with them, stinging like this?

"Ssssssss!" hissed the Nimbles, quite enjoying themselves.

"Snakes!" cried the goblins. "It's snakes! They've got snakes to protect them. We've been bitten by poisonous snakes! Oh, oh! We shall die of poison! Quick, go for help!"

The goblins fled away, their faces, hands and legs burning and smarting with nettle stings. Big white patches swelled up on them that hurt and stung.

"Good!" said Mr Nimble. "They've gone. How they yelled. Those nettles must have been very good stingers."

"They are," said one of the children. "One of them has given me a sting. I'll find a cool dock leaf and wrap it round my hand, then it will soon feel better. I expect the goblins have gone to a witch to be made better, and she will charge them a tremendous lot of money – but if they only knew it a few dock leaves would put them right!"

They delivered the necklace safely at the palace, and the Queen was very pleased. Then they went back home again, knowing they wouldn't meet any more goblins that night!

"It was a very good idea of yours, wife," said Mr Nimble. "A very good idea indeed."

So it was, wasn't it? And do you know what the Nimble children do now whenever they meet any of those mischievous goblins? They hiss just like snakes, and you should see those goblins rush away!

Rover's
Hide-and-Seek

Rover was a very clever dog indeed. He could balance biscuits or chocolates on his nose, toss them up into the air and catch them neatly in his mouth. He could shut the door and always waited for the click which told him it really was shut – and he could fetch Father's paper for him, and pay for it! He took the money in his mouth, and brought the paper back in his mouth too.

Another thing he could do was play hide-and-seek. You should have seen him! It was marvellous to watch him. He would stand behind a bush and wait patiently there while Mary or Peter hid themselves. He didn't shut his eyes – but he never looked round, because he wasn't a cheat.

Then when the two children had hidden themselves they would call "Cuckoo! Cuckoo!" Rover would at once bound away from the tree and go to look for the children! He always found them no matter where they hid. Father said he smelled where they went. He was really very clever.

He did love playing with Mary and Peter. Often he would go to their playroom and scrape at the door.

"Woof!" he said. "Woof!"

"There's Rover!" Mary would say. "He's come to ask us to play with him!

Come on, Peter. Let's play hide-and-seek!"

Now one day Mary and Peter went out for the day with their father. He wanted to take them to the zoo, and they were most excited.

"Can we take Rover too?" asked Peter. "He always comes with us, wherever we go, Daddy."

"No, we can't take him to the zoo," said Father. "Dogs are not allowed at the zoo. You wouldn't like him to fight a lion or a tiger, would you, Peter? Or try to make friends with a polar bear?"

"Well, Daddy, let's creep off without Rover knowing," said Mary. "He will be so upset if he sees us going off without him, really he will!"

So, while Rover was having a nice, crunchy breakfast of biscuits in the kitchen, the three slipped away out of the front door. Rover didn't know they had gone at all. He went on with his breakfast quite contentedly, planning to have a good game of hide-and-seek with Mary and Peter afterwards.

When he had finished he went upstairs to the playroom. He scraped at the door. He found that it was open a little so he went in. To his surprise there were no children in there. Wherever could they be? Downstairs, perhaps, trying to get a piece of cake from Mother!

So down went Rover and found Mother. But she was doing the ironing and she was rather cross.

"Shoo! Shoo!" she cried. "Get out Rover, I'm busy!"

Rover went into the garden, puzzled. Wherever in the world could those children be?

Then, as he stood by the old apple-tree, he heard a call:

"Cuckoo! Cuckoo!"

"Of course," thought Rover, his tail beginning to wag hard. "They're playing hide-and-seek! Why didn't I think of that? They are both hiding somewhere. I'll go and find them. I heard them calling cuckoo! It sounded as if it came from the end of the garden."

Down he trotted and smelled about by the wall there. But he could neither smell nor see the children. It was most puzzling. He held up his head and listened to see if he could hear them talking.

"Cuckoo! Cuckoo!" he heard.

"Tails and whiskers, that sounds as if they are up by the garden shed!" thought Rover, in surprise. "How could they have got from the bottom to the top of the garden without my seeing or hearing them?"

He ran to the garden shed, and looked inside and out. No children! No smell or sound of them either! It was really most strange. Rover couldn't understand it.

"Cuckoo! Cuckoo! Cuckoo!"

Rover listened in astonishment. Well, this time it sounded as if the children were calling to him from the front garden! He trotted there and hunted thoroughly. No, they were not there either!

Poor Rover! What a day of hide-and-seek he had, to be sure. You see he didn't know or guess that the cuckoo had come

back that day, and was calling merrily
all round about! He had quite forgotten
about that bird. He really and truly
thought it was the children calling him
as they always did when they played a
game of hide-and-seek with him.

By the time that Mary and Peter came
back Rover was quite tired out. He had
hunted everywhere, in all the places
where the cuckoo-call sounded to be
coming from. Mother could not think
what was the matter with Rover.

Whatever was he looking for, and why did he listen with his head on one side so often?

But when Peter and Mary came home from the zoo, and heard what Rover had been doing – and heard the cuckoo calling too – they guessed at once what had happened.

"Poor, darling old Rover!" said Mary, hugging him. "So you played hide-and-seek with the cuckoo all day long, did you, old fellow? What a shame! Never mind – we'll have a proper game tomorrow, and you really will find us this time!"

Rover wagged his tail. He was still very much puzzled – but nothing mattered now that he had his dear little master and mistress back again.

They played hide-and-seek the next day – but, you know, the cuckoo did spoil it for them. He *would* call cuckoo before they were ready! I think he must love to play hide-and-seek too – don't you?

The Little
Pixie-Cat

Once upon a time, Grubby the goblin did the Green Witch a good turn. In payment she gave him a little pixie-cat, and he carried it home in delight.

Now a pixie-cat is very valuable indeed, for it has plenty of magic in it. When it is exactly a year old it can turn all it sits upon to pure gold. Only just for that night, though, so that you must be sure to know the birthday of a pixie-cat or it is of no use to you.

Grubby the goblin was poor, and he was also very disagreeable. He was dirty and untidy, and none of his neighbours liked him, for he was always borrowing and never returning, always promising and never keeping his word.

So when they saw him carrying a pixie-cat home one day they didn't rush out and say how pleased they were. They just stared in surprise, and said to one another, "Ho! Grubby's got a pixie-cat! Perhaps he will wash himself for once on the cat's birthday!"

Grubby shut the cat in the cellar and went out to tell everyone of his good luck. He was angry that people didn't seem as glad as he wanted them to be. He went home frowning and scowling.

"Horrid things!" he said to himself. "They are jealous of me! They know I shall soon be rich. Indeed, I'll be so rich

that they'll have to make me Chief of the village – and won't I punish them and pay them back for all the rude things they have said to me and thought of me!"

The pixie-cat's first birthday was in three days' time, and the goblin became very busy, for he meant to be as rich as possible. He collected three sacks – one of pennies, one of stones and one of dust. Then he took a cushion and put it right on top of the three sacks.

"Ha!" he said, pleased with his idea. "On her birthday night the cat will sit on this cushion on top of these three sacks – and then when the clock strikes twelve the pennies will change to gold, the stones will be golden stones and the dust will be gold-dust, worth a fortune! Ho, I'll be richer than any goblin in the kingdom, and my, won't I make the people of this village sorry they ever looked down their noses at me!"

Now it was the custom for everyone in the village to be present on the first birthday of a pixie-cat, so that they might watch the wonderful magic working when the clock struck midnight. So Grubby the goblin sent out invitations, and at ten o'clock the people of the village began to arrive. There were pixies, brownies, gnomes, fairies and elves, and they all squeezed themselves into Grubby's little kitchen.

Grubby was there, and so was the pixie-cat, perched up high on her cushion, over the three sacks. Grubby hadn't provided any buns or lemonade – he was too mean. He just stood there and said "Good evening" when folk came in, but

he didn't say "How do you do?" or "It's a fine night" or anything polite and friendly. He really was an ill-mannered fellow.

At eleven o'clock everyone was there. Then Grubby began to talk. How he talked! How he boasted! And dear me, what a spiteful, mean little goblin he showed himself to be.

"Nobody's ever had a pixie-cat in this village except me!" he said. "I'm going to be rich – richer than any of you. I shall build myself a new cottage with six rooms, and I shall have two servants. I shall give wonderful feasts to all the witches and goblins I know – but I shan't ask any of you to my feasts! No, I shall leave you out!"

"We shan't mind that, Grubby," said a tall brownie. "You don't wash your neck often enough for us to want to come to your parties!"

"Ho, is that you, Skinny the brownie?" cried the goblin fiercely. "Well, let me tell you this – I'll buy your cottage when I'm rich, and I'll turn you out, you and

all your children – so there!"

"You always were a mean fellow," said an elf with long silver wings. "You'll be more horrid than ever when you are rich!"

"You'll never be rich!" shouted Grubby angrily. "You play about with butterflies and birds all day long, Silverwings! They can't do anything for you. Why don't you make friends with witches, as I do? Then maybe you would have a pixie-cat too, to make you rich."

"We don't want to be rich," said a gnome. "We are quite happy as we are. Your gold won't make you any happier, Grubby; don't make any mistake about that. It won't make us like you any better, or be any more friendly. We'd rather be friends with a lame earwig than with a rich and unpleasant goblin like you!"

Grubby was so angry that he hardly knew what to say. For a while everyone sat silent, watching the hands of the clock creeping slowly round to midnight.

The little pixie-cat began to purr loudly. She knew it was nearly time for her magic to work.

Grubby became excited as he saw the time getting so near. He began to talk again.

"When all these sacks hold gold," he said, "I shall buy a golden carriage and ride in it. I shall wear a cloak of silver cloth, and lace my shoes with golden laces. I shall ask the Great Wizard who lives in Towering Castle to visit me. And I will walk through the village with him, pretending not to see you."

Grubby took up his walking-stick and pretended he was walking down the street, looking haughtily from side to side.

"When I meet any of you on the path, I shall say: 'Get out of my way!'," he said, "and if you don't move at once, I shall hit you with my stick! Like that! And like that!"

Grubby slashed about in the air with his stick, and the pixie-cat stopped purring in alarm. It was almost twelve o'clock, but Grubby still had one more thing to say.

"And the Great Wizard from Towering Castle will wave his stick round his head, and change you all into earwigs – like this!"

Grubby swung his stick sharply round his head and the end of it hit the little pixie-cat on the cushion! She gave a sharp mew, sprang fiercely at Grubby, and scratched his arm. Then she leaped out of the window and disappeared into the night. At the same moment the clock began to strike twelve!

"Oh, oh! I'm hurt! The pixie-cat's gone and it's midnight! Catch her, someone!" groaned the goblin. But nobody moved. Everyone was thinking exactly the same thought.

"It serves Grubby the goblin right!" they all thought. And so it did. Silently the little folk slipped out of the cottage and went home, leaving Grubby alone.

How ashamed he was! How he cried and groaned! He felt as if he couldn't possibly face anyone the next day, so he

packed up his bag and went. Where he journeyed to, nobody knows, and nobody wants to know either!

As for that little pixie-cat, she went back to the Green Witch, and there she is still. The little folk saw the way she went, because all the stones and earth she ran on as the clock struck midnight changed into gold. They left the gold patches there as a warning to greedy goblins, and you can see them to this day – curious yellow spots in the ground, the size of a little cat's footprint!

Conceited
Caroline

Caroline was a doll – and goodness, what a marvellous doll she was! She wore a beautiful blue dress, a wonderful coat to match, blue shoes and socks and a little hat that was so full of flowers it looked like a little garden.

It was her hat that every one admired so much. There were daisies, buttercups, cornflowers, poppies, and grass round the hat, and it suited Caroline perfectly. She knew this, so she always wore her hat, even when she played games with the toys.

"You are vain, Caroline!" said the panda teasingly.

That made Caroline go red. She *was* vain, and she knew it. She knew she was pretty. She knew that her clothes were lovely. She knew that her flowery hat was the prettiest one the toys had ever seen, and that it made her look really sweet.

"I'm not vain!" said Caroline. "Not a bit!"

"You are! You're conceited and stuck-up," said the teddy-bear, who always said what he thought. "Why, you even wear your hat when you play with us. And if we play a bit roughly you turn up your nose and say, 'Oh please! You'll tear my pretty dress!' Pooh! Conceited Caroline!"

Caroline was angry. She glared at the bear and then she walked straight up to him. She took hold of his pink bow and tugged it. It came undone and Caroline pulled it off. And then she tore the ribbon in half. Wasn't she naughty?

"Oh! You horrid doll! Look what you have done! You've torn my ribbon and now I can't tie it round my neck, and I shall show where my head is sewn on to my body," wept the bear.

"Well, it just serves you right," said Caroline, and she walked off.

And after that the toys wouldn't have anything to do with Caroline. They wouldn't play with her. They wouldn't talk to her. They wouldn't even speak when she called to them. So Caroline was cross and unhappy.

One night, when the children were asleep and the toys came alive to play, Caroline took off her beautiful flowery hat and hung it up in the playhouse. She thought perhaps the toys might play with her if she didn't wear her hat. She fluffed out her curly hair and gazed at the panda.

"Ho!" said the panda. "Now you want to show off your curly hair, I suppose! Well, go and show it to the table and the chair and the curtains! We don't want to see it, Conceited Caroline!"

So that wasn't any use. Caroline went to a corner and sulked. She was very angry. How dare the toys take no notice of her, the prettiest doll in the whole playroom!

Then the toys planned a party. It was the birthday of the clockwork mouse and everyone loved him because he was such a dear. So they thought they would have a party for him, and games, and gave him a lovely time.

But they didn't ask Caroline. The teddy cooked some exciting cakes and biscuits on the stove in the play house, and the panda cut up a rosy apple into slices. The toys set out the chairs round the little wooden table and put the dishes and plates ready.

Everything looked so nice. "It's a pity that we can't put a vase of flowers in the middle of the table," said the panda. "I always think flowers look so sweet at a party. Come along, everyone – we'll just go and tidy ourselves up and then the party can begin."

They all went to find the brush and comb in the toy-cupboard. Caroline went to look at the birthday-table and thought that it looked lovely with its cakes and biscuits and apple-slices.

"I do wish I had something to give the clockwork mouse," thought Caroline. "I

do love him. He's such a dear. But I expect he would throw it back at me if I had anything to give. The toys are so horrid to me now."

And then Caroline suddenly had a marvellous idea. What about her flowery hat? Couldn't she take the flowers off that beautiful hat and put them into a vase for the middle of the birthday-table? They would look really sweet.

She rushed to get her hat. She took the flowers off it. She found a little vase and began to put them in – buttercups, daisies, cornflowers, poppies, and the grass. You can't think how sweet they looked.

Caroline popped the vase of flowers in the middle of the table and went back to her corner. She looked at her hat rather sadly. It looked very strange without its flowers. She would look funny if she wore it any more.

The toys ran to the birthday-table to begin the party – and how they stared when they saw the lovely flowers in the middle of the table!

"Where did they come from?" cried the panda in astonishment.

"Oh, what a lovely surprise for me!" cried the clockwork mouse. And then he guessed who had put the flowers for him.

"It's Caroline – they are the flowers from her hat!" he squeaked. "Oh, Caroline, thank you! Do come to my party!"

"Yes, do come!" cried all the toys. And the panda ran and took her hand.

"If you can give up the flowers you were so proud of, you can't be so horrid after all!" he cried. "Come along, Caroline, and join the party."

So Caroline went and everyone was so nice to her that she was quite happy again. Sometimes she wears her hat without the flowers, and do you know what the toys say? They say, "Why, Caroline, you look just as nice without the flowers – you really do!"

And so she does!

Christmas
at Last!

"Christmas is coming," said Bobs to Bimbo and Topsy. Bobs was a black-and-white fox terrier.

"Who's he?" asked Topsy, the fox terrier puppy. "A visitor?"

"No, silly," said Bobs. "Christmas is a day – we all get presents and everyone is happy."

"Who brings the presents?" asked Bimbo.

"Santa Claus, of course," said Bobs.

"Any relation of mine?" asked Bimbo, the naughty Siamese kitten, stretching out his twenty claws for everyone to see. "I'm Bimbo Claws, as you can see. Is Santa Claus an uncle of mine, do you think?"

"Don't be funny," said Bobs. "Santa

Claus is a kind old gentleman. Gillian and Imogen call up the chimney to tell him what they want in their Christmas stockings. They hang up a stocking each, and Santa Claus fills it on Christmas Eve. We had better hang up stockings too. It would be lovely to find bones and chews and biscuits in them, wouldn't it!"

"That seems a very good idea," said Bimbo, sitting up. "Did you say this nice old gentleman lives up the chimney?"

"No, I didn't," said Bobs. "I said that the children call up the chimney to tell him what they want."

"Well, if he can hear them, he must be up the chimney then," said Topsy. "Bimbo, you're used to chimneys. You climb up them all, one by one, and see which one Santa Claus lives in."

"No thank you," said Bimbo. "No more chimneys for me. We'll call up, though, and say what we want, shall we?"

"And we'll hang up stockings too," said Cosy, the tabby cat.

"We haven't got any," said Topsy. "We

don't wear them. Can't we hang up our collars instead?"

"I suppose you think our collars would easily hold things like biscuits and chews," said Bobs. "I do think you are silly sometimes, Topsy."

"Well, you be clever and tell us what to do about stockings then," said Topsy, snapping at Bobs's tail.

"Don't do that," said Bobs. "Let me think a minute. Oh, I know!"

"What?" cried Topsy, Bimbo and Cosy.

"Well, you know that the children's socks are hung up on the line to dry, don't you?" said Bobs. "Well, what about jumping up and getting some for ourselves? We can easily do that!"

So the next day all four of them went to look at the clothes-line. And, sure enough, there were two pairs of long socks there, one belonging to Imogen and one to Gillian. It wasn't long before Bobs was jumping up to get hold of one.

But he couldn't get high enough. So Cosy tried. She caught hold of a sock with her claws. She hung on for all she was worth and, oh dear, the clothes-line broke, and all the clothes fell in a heap on poor Cosy!

How scared she was! She tore off down the garden, with the line wound round her body and all the clothes galloped after her!

It was the funniest sight to see. Bobs, Topsy and Bimbo sat down and laughed till they cried. But when their mistress came out and saw how all the clean clothes had been dragged in the mud, she wasn't a bit pleased. Cosy got a scolding and sat and sulked all by herself in the corner.

"That was a very bad idea of yours," she said to Bobs.

But when Christmas Eve came, what a lovely surprise! Gillian and Imogen came into the playroom with four stockings and showed them to the surprised animals.

"You shall hang up your stockings just as we do!" said Imogen. "Here is one for you, Bobs, and one for you, Topsy, and smaller ones for the cats."

The four stockings were hung just above the animals' baskets. They did look funny, hanging limp and thin and empty.

"If you go to sleep, and don't peep, perhaps Santa Claus will come down the chimney here in the night and fill these stockings for you," said Imogen. "Perhaps you will have a new collar, Bobs – and you a rubber bone, Topsy – and you a ball to roll about, Bimbo – and you a new rug for your basket, Cosy. And maybe you will have biscuits and sardines and bones and other nice things as well! So go to sleep and don't make a sound, in case you frighten Santa Claus away!"

"Isn't this exciting?" said Topsy, when the children had gone out of the room. "I'm going to settle down in my basket and go to sleep straight away!"

"So am I," said Bimbo. "Oooh, I do hope I shall get a tin of sardines. I wonder if Santa Claus will have any in his sack?"

"I really would love a new collar," said Bobs. "Mine is so old. Well – goodnight to you all. I'm going to sleep too. And if we hear old Father Christmas, we mustn't peep! Do you hear, Topsy? No peeping!"

"Well, don't you peep either," said Topsy. "And don't think he is a robber or something when he comes, and bark at him, or you'll frighten him away! Goodnight, everyone!"

And very soon all the animals were fast asleep. Bobs and Cosy were curled up together in one big basket, and Bimbo and Topsy were fast asleep in the small one.

They dreamed that their stockings were full of all the things that animals love, bones and biscuits, sardines and kippers, balls and saucers of cream!

In the morning the four animals awoke. Topsy woke first and put her head out of the basket. She sniffed hard. She could smell a lovely smell.

"Oh! It's Christmas morning!" she wuffed in Bimbo's ear. Bimbo woke up with a jump.

"What about our stockings?" he said. "Did Santa Claus come in the night and

fill them? I didn't hear him."

"Look!" cried Bobs, waking up too.
"Our stockings are crammed full! I can
smell bones."

"And I can smell sardines!" cried Cosy.
All the animals got out of their baskets
and sniffed round the exciting stockings.

"A new collar for me!" barked Bobs,
dragging one out in delight. "Just look

at it; brass studs all the way round. My goodness, I shall look grand. I wish I had a tie to go with it, like men wear."

"A rubber bone for me!" wuffed Topsy, and she took the bone from her stocking and tried to chew it. But the more she chewed at the bone, the less she seemed to eat of it. Most peculiar!

"That bone will last you for years," said Bobs with a grin. "It's all chew and no taste! Give me a real bone any day!"

"A fine new ball for me!" mewed Bimbo, rolling a lovely red ball over the floor. "Come and play with me, Topsy. Throw it into the air and make it bounce."

"What about my new rug?" said Cosy, dragging a knitted rug into her basket and lying down on it. "Now this is what I call a really nice present. I shall be able to lie on it and keep myself warm, and you, Bobs, will be able to hide all kinds of goodies under it, to keep till you want them."

"What, hide them under your rug for you to nibble at when I'm not there!"

cried Bobs. "No, thank you, Cosy. Oh, tails and whiskers, there are other things in our stockings too! A real big bone for me, full of crunch and nibble!"

"And there's a tin of sardines for me and Bimbo," said Cosy. "Oh, I hope Gillian and Imogen come along quickly to open it. I just feel as if I could do with three or four sardines inside me."

"There are biscuits at the bottom of *my* stocking," said Topsy, putting her head right down to the bottom of the stocking and nosing about in the toe.

"Biscuits! Big ones and little ones! I'll give you each one if you like."

She got some in her mouth, but, dear me, when she wanted to take out her head and give the biscuits to the others, she couldn't get rid of the stocking. It stuck fast over her head and Topsy ran about the room in the stocking. The others did laugh!

Then in came Gillian and Imogen. "Happy Christmas, Bobs, Topsy, Bimbo and Cosy!" they cried. "Oh, Topsy, whatever are you doing? What are you wearing that stocking on your head for? Did you think it was a hat?"

They pulled the stocking from Topsy's head, and the four animals crowded round the children to thank them for their lovely presents. Topsy was glad to have her head out of the stocking.

"Here's a bar of chocolate for you two girls," said Bobs, and he pulled one out from his basket. "I've sat on it for the last week, I'm afraid, so it's a bit squashy, but the taste is still there, because I've tried it each morning."

"And here's one of my very best biscuits," said Topsy, fetching one from her basket. "It's the biggest one I have had in my dinner bowl for weeks. Try it. I've nibbled a pattern all round the edge to make it pretty for you."

"And I've been into the hen-run and collected you a few feathers," said Cosy. "I hope they'll be useful. Good gracious, Bimbo – whatever have you got there?"

"My collection of kipper-heads from the rubbish-heaps all round," said Bimbo proudly. "They're the best I could find. I hid them in the landing cupboard in a hatbox there."

"Gracious! That was what made that awful smell, I suppose!" said Gillian. "And, oh dear, Bimbo, Mummy keeps one of her best hats in that box. I can't imagine what she'll say if she goes out smelling of kippers."

"I should think she'll be very pleased," said Bimbo. "Kippers have a gorgeous smell. I'm surprised people don't make scent of them, instead of silly things like honeysuckle and sweet-peas!"

"Well, thank you all very much," said Gillian. "You've given us lovely presents. Now let's all go to breakfast, and we'll show you the presents we had too!"

So off they all went, Bobs wearing his new collar, and Topsy carrying her rubber bone for another long chew. Cosy had to leave her rug behind, but Bimbo rolled his ball all the way to the dining-room.

The sardines were opened, and Cosy and Bimbo shared them with the dogs.

"Delicious," they all said, and licked their whiskers clean.

They had a lovely Christmas, and even

had a taste of the great big turkey. They had a special supper that evening of biscuits soaked in turkey gravy, and then, full of good things, they all went to their baskets to sleep.

They curled up together, put their noses between their paws, and dreamed lovely dreams of sardines, bones, collars and balls! And there we will leave them, dreaming happily.

Mr Stamp-About's Hat

Mr Stamp-About was feeling rather pleased with himself. He had actually been in a good temper for a whole morning!

"I'll just go for my walk now, before it's time for my lunch," he said to himself. "Where's my lovely new hat? I'll put it on this morning, and go smiling down the street, so that everyone can see I'm really a very pleasant fellow."

So away he went, wearing his new hat a little on one side, with such a broad smile on his face that he astonished everyone he met.

"Hello – what's up with you this morning, Stamp-About?" said Jinky, in surprise. "I don't believe I ever saw you without a frown before. You look as though you lost tenpence and found a pound. What's happened?"

"No. But it sounds a very good idea," said Stamp-About, and began to look on the ground. He hummed a little tune as he went and when Mrs Bonnet met him, she could hardly believe her ears. Stamp-About humming a song – well, well, such a thing had surely never happened before!

"I didn't know you could hum a tune," she said. "I thought you could only shout and yell, Stamp-About."

"Well, you're wrong," said Stamp-About. "How do you like my new hat?"

"It's nice – but I like your new face better," said Mrs Bonnet. "Now see you keep that smile, Stamp-About, and go on humming your little tune. Before you know where you are you'll be a really nice fellow!"

"If nobody annoys me, I'll annoy nobody," said Stamp-About. "I'm only cross when people treat me badly."

"Oh rubbish!" said Mrs Bonnet, giving him a little poke with her umbrella. "You love to show a bit of temper, Stamp-About, you love to shout and rage, you know you do. There now, look – you're frowning already! What did I tell you?"

Stamp-About made himself smile, though he was already beginning to feel cross with Mrs Bonnet. He raised his hat, said goodbye, and went on, longing to jab Mrs Bonnet with his stick, just as she had poked him with her umbrella. Horrid woman!

"Now, now – I musn't think nasty things this morning, when I feel so pleased to be wearing a new hat," he thought, and he smiled again. Everyone was most surprised, and some of the people he met smiled back at him. Stamp-About began to feel he must be a very nice person indeed.

He heard the sound of shouting and cheering as he turned the corner, and saw a circus procession coming along – vans, carts, cages on wheels – what fun! The big village policeman stood nearby, waving it on its way.

"Get along now! Don't stop here, you'll make a crowd collect!" he shouted. "Keep on your way, that's right. Oh – hello, Mr Stamp-About. What's the matter with you this morning? You don't look yourself! Good gracious me, you're smiling!"

"I just happen to feel in a very good temper, that's all," said Mr Stamp-About. "Can't I smile if I want to?"

"Dear me, yes. It just gave me a surprise that's all, to see your face with a smile," said the policeman. "I hope this means you've turned over a new leaf, Mr Stamp-About. I had a lot of complaints about you last week – shouting at little Tommy Brown, and chasing Sally Prim, and stamping your foot at old Mr Tremble. In fact, I was going to come along and march you off to the police station, the very next complaint I had."

"I tell you, I'm in a very good temper today," said Stamp-About crossly, frowning at the policeman.

"Ah – now you look more like yourself, frowning all over your face like that,"

said the policeman. "But mind what I say now – any more shouting and stamping from you, and I'll be after you!" He waved on the circus procession as he spoke.

Mr Stamp-About wanted to stamp his foot at the policeman, but he remembered that he was in a very good temper and decided not to. He gave him a sudden scowl, changed it quickly to a sudden smile, and turned away. He tilted his fine new hat a little more to one side, and went across the road.

He stood under a tree there, watching the procession – ah, here came a cage of mischievous little monkeys and now came a clown, turning head-over-heels, and look at that lovely horse, with a little girl standing on its back, blowing kisses to everyone! Stamp-About actually blew a kiss back to her!

And then, quite suddenly, his hat disappeared from his head! One moment it was there, on Stamp-About's big head – the next it was gone! He stood there bare-headed, gaping in surprise, running his hand through his hair.

"My hat! Where's it gone? Who's taken it?" he said, staring all round angrily. A small girl laughed suddenly. She had seen who had taken it!

A monkey had escaped from the circus cage, and had leaped up into the tree under which Stamp-About stood. When the little creature looked down, he saw the fine new hat and straightaway the rascal reached down a paw, and whipped it off, racing to the top of the tree with it. Only the little girl had seen him, and she laughed and laughed, pointing at Stamp-About's angry face.

"Your hat's gone!" she cried.

"Who took it? Wait till I catch him!" shouted Stamp-About, and looked all round. He yelled into the ear of the man standing next to him. "Where's my hat? Did you see it go?"

"You're deafening me," said the man, moving away, annoyed. "How do I know about your hat? I expect it blew off in the wind. Go and shout in someone else's ear, not mine!"

"Who saw it blow away?" shouted Stamp-About. "Here, you – little girl! Did you see it blow away?"

"No. But I saw it go!" said the little girl laughing. "Oh, how cross you look!"

Stamp-About saw something being blown along by the wind, down the street, and he rushed after it. But it wasn't his hat – it was just an old cardboard box.

"My new hat! This would happen!" said Stamp-About, angrily, looking all round. "Ah – there's a man hurrying round the corner and it looks as if he's holding my lovely new hat in his hand. Hey! stop! I want my hat!"

He raced after the man, rushed round the corner and bumped straight into a woman with a basket of shopping. A bag shot out of her basket, and landed on Stamp-About's foot. *Crash!* Six new-laid eggs burst all over his leg!

"Now then – look where you're going! You've broken my eggs!" cried the woman, angrily. "I'll tell the policeman about you. Hey, come back!"

But Stamp-About was now halfway down the road, still chasing the man. He caught up with him, and clutched him by the shoulder. "Give me my hat!" he shouted. "It's my new one. How dare you steal it off my head?"

And then he saw that the man wasn't carrying a hat after all, but a big black cat. The cat was frightened and shot out its claws. *Scratch!* It dug them into Stamp-About's hand, and he hopped about in pain.

"I'll have that cat put in prison!" he shouted. "How dare you carry a dangerous animal like that about in the street?"

"Well, I like that! You're much more dangerous than my poor old cat!" said the man, angrily. "What do you mean by . . ."

But now Stamp-About had spied

another man, this time wearing a fine big hat, very like the one he had lost, and he was racing after him, shouting loudly.

"Stop! Stop! I can see you! Stop thief, and give me my new hat!"

The man was shocked and frightened to see Stamp-About racing after him, shouting and waving his fists. He thought he must be quite mad! He began to run fast. "If only I can find a policeman," thought the man. "Whatever is the matter with that fellow? Goodness me, he might hit me with that stick he's waving!"

The man raced round a corner, and then up the next street, trying to see the policeman. After him came Stamp-About, quite sure that the man had stolen his hat. Wasn't he running away? Didn't that mean he had got his hat and meant to keep it?

The man saw the circus procession in the distance, and tore after it. Ah, good – there was the village policeman. He panted up to him.

"Oh, Constable! Arrest this idiot who is chasing me! I saw him upset a woman's shopping – and then he raced after me, howling like a madman!"

The policeman was most astonished to see Stamp-About rushing up, looking as fierce as could be. "Hey, Constable! Arrest that man – he's stolen my new hat and what's more, he's wearing it!" shouted Stamp-About. The man clutched his hat, and glared at Stamp-About.

"It is *not* your hat. It's got my name inside. Constable, shall I show you?"

"Yes," said the astonished policeman, and took the hat from the angry man.

Sure enough, there was his name inside – Mr Tom Trotty. Stamp-About saw it too and stared in surprise.

The little girl who had seen the monkey ran up and whispered into the policeman's ear. He smiled.

"Mr Stamp-About, this little girl says she can show you who is wearing your hat, and if you like to take it from him, you can," he said. "But I'm afraid I'll have to take *you* – to the police station! Didn't I warn you what would happen if you lost your temper again? I thought that smile of yours wouldn't last out the morning!"

"Oh, stop your talking – where is my hat, and who's got it?" shouted Stamp-About, stamping his foot so hard that he hurt himself. "I'll soon catch him, if you don't!"

"Look up there," said the little girl, with a giggle – and everyone looked up into the tree she pointed to. There sat the monkey, with Stamp-About's hat on his head, tilted to one side, grinning all over his cheeky face.

"It suits him," said the policeman. "It suits him better than it suited you, Stamp-About. Well, go and get it, if you want it. I can't arrest a little monkey!"

But as soon as Stamp-About began to climb the tree, shouting with temper, the monkey leaped into the next tree, down the trunk, and then scampered along the road after the circus procession – still wearing the hat! How everyone laughed!

Well, Stamp-About couldn't catch him and he never saw his hat again. But *I* know what happened to it! The monkey gave it to the ring-master and he wears that lovely new top hat whenever he goes into the ring and cracks his great whip!

Stamp-About was very angry, but nobody was sorry. "You've lost something else, as well as your hat," said the policeman, looking solemnly at him. "Better try and find it, Stamp-About. Look in all your pockets!"

So Stamp-About turned out his pockets. Whatever had he lost? Everyone watched, nudging one another and laughing.

"I haven't lost anything except my hat," said Stamp-About at last, and he stamped his foot. "You're not telling the truth. My money's here – and my watch – and my notebook – and my handkerchief. I haven't lost anything!"

"You have," said the policeman. "Tell him what he's lost, everyone!" So they told him.

"Your temper, Stamp-About – your temper!" they shouted – and you should have seen him stamp away in a mighty rage! No wonder he couldn't find it in his pockets!

Oona-Rilly,
Oona-Roo

"Look, what the puppy has done to the little floating duck!" said the teddy. "He's bitten a hole in him!"

"Oh, dear!" said Janie, the smallest doll. "Quack, do you feel all right?"

"No, not quite," said Quack. "I'm dreadfully afraid that I won't be able to float in the bathwater any more – then Sam won't take me in his bath. I shall fill with water and sink, you see!"

"Yes. I remember he had a toy goldfish called Finny, once," said the teddy. "And Finny got a hole in, and sank in the bath. Sam threw him away into the dustbin."

"Oh, don't say things like that!" said Quack. "Can't you do something to help me?"

"Well – first let's make sure that you

can't float any more," said Janie the doll.

"You're not thinking of filling the bath for that, are you?" said the teddy, in surprise. "I don't believe any of us could turn on the tap!"

"We couldn't – and anyway, I'm not thinking of that," said Janie. "We'll pop Quack on the water in the goldfish bowl. The goldfish won't mind. Then, if he fills with water we'll know that somehow or other we've got to help him."

So they carried Quack up to the table, and put him into the goldfish bowl. He floated quite well for a while – but then water began to seep into the hole where the puppy had bitten him, and soon he began to sink, because he was full of water!

"Catch him before he goes right under!" cried Janie, and the teddy lifted him out just in time. He tipped him up so that the water could run out of the hole.

"You see – I won't be of use to Sam any more," said poor Quack. "What can I do?"

"I'm going to call in the brownie who

lives outside our window," said Janie.

"Oh, yes!" said the teddy. "You sewed on some of his buttons for him the other day, didn't you – and he said he'd do you a good turn one day!"

"That's why I'm going to call him in," said Janie. "I'm ready for his good turn – but I want it passed on to little Quack."

She went to the window and put her head out through the crack at the bottom, where it was open. She called softly. "Brownie! Please come, I want your help."

The ivy leaves stirred, and a tiny bearded face looked out. It was a small brownie who had made quite a comfortable home for himself in an old blackbird's nest.

"Hello, Janie! What do you want?" he said.

"Do you know a way of mending the hole in Quack?" she asked him.

"I'll come and see," said the brownie, and in a second he was down in the playroom. He pulled his long beard and frowned when he saw the hole.

"First we must fill it up with something," he said. "Clay would do. Anybody got a bit of clay?" Nobody had.

Then the toy dog spoke in his wuffy voice. "I know where there's some – those long coloured sticks in the box over there are clay."

"No, that's Plasticine," said the teddy.

"It's coloured clay," said the dog. "Isn't it, Brownie?"

The brownie went to look at it. "Yes – this will do fine," he said. "I'll take a bit of yellow to match Quack's body."

98

So he snipped off a tiny bit of yellow Plasticine and rolled it between his hands to soften it. When it was nice and soft and flat he went to Quack.

"I shan't hurt you," he said. "Just keep quite still for a minute, please."

The brownie pressed the yellow clay hard on to the hole in the duck's body. Then he smoothed it nicely. "Does that feel all right?" he asked.

"Oh, yes – I feel quite well again now,"

said Quack, pleased. "Will it be sure to stop the water from coming in, Brownie?"

"It should," said the brownie. "But to make quite certain, please keep still while I stroke it with the feather out of my hat, and say a very magic word. Silence, please."

Everyone was quiet. The brownie took the long feather from his cap, and stroked the filled-up hole in Quack's body.

"Oona-rilly, oona-roo," he said, three times over. "There! That should be quite all right now!"

Well, you know, it was! When Sam floated Quack on his bath that night, the little duck bobbed on the ripples just as merrily as ever, and no water soaked into his body at all! He was so pleased.

You'll know what to do if your bath-toys get a hole in them. You might as well use the magic word, too, three times over. You're not a brownie, but it would be fun to see if there's any magic about!

My Goodness, What a Joke!

One day Mrs Well-I-Never came rushing to speak to her brother, Grabbit the gnome.

"Grabbit!" she said. "Where are you? I've got news for you! Look what I've found."

"What?" asked Grabbit disagreeably. "You always find such silly things, stones with holes in, or four-leaved clovers that aren't lucky, or things that belong to someone else!"

"Well, you just see what I've got!" said Mrs Well-I-Never, and she opened her hand and showed something to Grabbit. It was a tiny box of blue powder.

"It's a blue spell!" said Mrs Well-I-Never. "Dame Dandy must have dropped it on her way up the hill this morning.

It's the same kind of spell that she put in her cauldron on the day you fell into it and came out blue. Don't you remember?"

"I'm hardly likely to forget while my nose is still blue," said Grabbit gloomily. "Throw the spell away, Sister, I don't like blue spells."

"No, but listen," said Mrs Well-I-Never. "You know we've always wanted to pay little Shuffle back for making you fall into Dame Dandy's blue spell? Well, now we've got a wonderful way to get even with him."

"How?" said surly Grabbit.

"Do listen, Grabbit," said Mrs Well-I-Never. "I'll make a cake, and I'll put this blue spell into it, and I'll send it along to Ma Shuffle because it is her birthday! She'll eat it and so will Shuffle, and they'll both turn blue!"

"Ha ha, ho ho!" roared Grabbit suddenly. "That's a good joke. Oh, that's the best joke I ever heard. Make your cake, quickly!"

So Mrs Well-I-Never made the cake. It was a beauty, crammed with fruit. She shook the blue powder into it and baked it. "It's a pity I can't ice it," she said. "I haven't any icing sugar."

"Oh, never mind about that," said Grabbit. "Is it ready? Well, take it down to Ma Shuffle at once. Ho, ho, what will she and little Shuffle look like tomorrow? Oh, what a joke this is, what a joke!"

"Well, I never! I've not seen you so pleased for years!" said his sister. "Well, I'll go now. And don't you give our secret away to anyone!"

Ma Shuffle was surprised and pleased

with Mrs Well-I-Never's present of a cake. "Thank you," she said. "Do come to my party this afternoon and share the cake, will you?"

"Oh, no, thank you," said Mrs Well-I-Never at once. "That would never do! Well, happy birthday, Ma!"

"Look at that," said Ma to little Shuffle. "There's kindness even in Mrs Well-I-Never. What a pity she sent me a cake though – I've such an enormous one already, and it's iced so beautifully."

"Ma, send Mrs Well-I-Never's cake to Mrs Nearby," said Shuffle. "We've got enough cake, really, and it's nice to be generous if we can. Mrs Nearby can't come to your party, she's not well. She'd love a cake for herself!"

"Bless your kind heart, little Shuffle," said Ma. "You take it along then, with my best wishes."

So the blue spell cake was taken over to Mrs Nearby's by little Shuffle. Mrs Nearby was in bed and couldn't come to the door, so Shuffle pushed the cake in through the window.

"Thank you, little Shuffle, you're kind," said Mrs Nearby. "I'm expecting the doctor soon, and maybe he'll tell me I can get up."

The doctor did come, very soon after that. He was Doctor Healem, and he was just like his name. He shook his head over Mrs Nearby.

"No, you can't get up yet," he said. "And what's this rich fruit cake I see here on the windowsill? You mustn't eat anything like that yet, Mrs Nearby."

"Oh dear, well, will you take it away

and give it to someone?" said Mrs Nearby. "I might nibble a bit if you don't, it looks so good."

"Yes, I'll take it to Mrs Shifty," said Doctor Healem, and he took it away with him. But Mrs Shifty was out, so he left the cake just by the front door. She found it there when she came home.

"Look at that! Somebody has left a cake here for me!" she said. "Well, I'd keep it, only I'm going away tomorrow and it would get stale in my larder. I'd better give it away."

So what did she do but take it that very afternoon to Mrs Button. Mrs Button was pleased.

"Well, that's nice of you," she said. "I'll let little Button have it for his tea. I don't like fruit cake myself, so he can eat it all. He'll start off with five or six slices, I expect!"

But little Button was very naughty that afternoon. "Now you just shan't have that beautiful cake!" scolded Mrs Button. "I'm ashamed of you, spoiling your nice new coat like that! Don't you know wet paint when you see it? Don't you—"

"All right, Ma, all right," said Button. "I won't have the cake. Don't go on and on at me though! What shall I do with the cake?"

"You take it to Mrs Popalong," said Ma Button. "Go along now – and don't you go near that wet paint on the way!"

Button went to Mrs Popalong's. She was very busy baking. "Mrs Popalong, I've brought you something from Ma!" called Button.

"Put it down on the hall table," called back Mrs Popalong. "I'm busy this morning, little Button. You put it there and I'll see to it when I've finished."

So Button left the cake on the hall table, and when Mrs Popalong came along to see what he had left, she laughed aloud.

"Well, I would get a present of a cake just when it's my baking day and I've made six!" she said. "It's a nice enough cake, too – but it looks a bit battered somehow, round the top. I'll ice it when I ice mine and send if off to someone else. I know Pa Popalong won't eat any cakes but mine, so it's no good keeping this one!"

Well, she iced it beautifully in pink and white and put pink roses on top. Now, who should she send it to? Everyone was going to Ma Shuffle's party this afternoon – but wait! Didn't she hear Ma say that Mrs Well-I-Never and Grabbit weren't going? Well, she'd send them the cake then! They'd be glad of it, if they were missing the party.

So kind Mrs Popalong walked to Mrs Well-I-Never's house and offered her the iced cake. Mrs Well-I-Never was thrilled to see it.

"Well, I never!" she said. "I never did see such a fine cake. Did you ice it yourself, Mrs Popalong?"

"Yes," said Mrs Popalong. "But I didn't make the cake. I don't know who made it – little Button brought it along this morning. Well, I hope you enjoy it, Mrs Well-I-Never!"

"Grabbit!" called Mrs Well-I-Never that teatime. "Come and have tea. Mrs Popalong's sent a fine iced cake for us!"

"Oh, good!" said Grabbit, and he sat down at the table. "My, it certainly is a fine-looking cake. I say, Sister, do you suppose little Shuffle and his ma are sitting down gobbling up that blue spell cake?"

"Yes!" said Mrs Well-I-Never. "Oh, what a joke! I'm glad I'm not having a bit!"

"I'm glad too," said Grabbit, taking his second slice of cake. "It's the best

joke I ever heard in my life. Ha ha, ho ho
ho! What a joke!"

Well, it was, of course – but not quite in
the way they meant. By the end of
teatime they were both as blue as
cornflowers!

My goodness, what a joke!

The
Three Wishes

Emma and Bobby were sitting in the meadow and, as usual, they were quarrelling.

They were brother and sister, but to hear them quarrelling with one another, you might have thought they were enemies!

"I didn't want to come to this wood. I wanted to go up the hill," said Emma. "You always do what you want. You never do what I want."

"Oh, you fibber!" said Bobby. "You are the most selfish girl I know – I am always having to do what you choose. I don't like you a bit."

"Well, I don't like—" Emma began, and then she stopped. She had seen something moving in the buttercups near her. She put out her hand quickly and caught the thing that was moving.

To her enormous surprise, it was a pixie! The little creature gave a scream, and wriggled hard. But Emma didn't let go, she held the pixie very tightly.

"Look!" she said to Bobby, in an excited voice. "Look! I've caught a fairy!"

"Let me go!" squealed the little thing. "You're hurting me."

"Make her give us three wishes," said Bobby, suddenly. "Go on – tell her. Then we might get three wishes that would come true!"

Emma squeezed the poor little pixie till she cried out.

"Give us three wishes and I'll let you go," she said. "Three wishes! Then we can make ourselves rich and happy and wise."

"I'll give you three wishes," said the pixie. "But they won't do you any good! Children like you can't wish for the right things! But I'll give you three wishes if you want them."

Emma let the pixie go, and the little thing fled away among the buttercups, laughing as if she had heard a joke.

"What's she laughing at?" said Bobby. "Oh, well, never mind. Now what shall we wish?"

"I want to wish for a budgerigar that can talk," said Emma, at once. "I've always wanted one."

"What a silly wish!" said Bobby. "No – let's wish for a little aeroplane that will take us anywhere we want to go."

"I'm sure I don't want to fly in the air with you as the pilot," said Emma. "No, you're not to wish for that."

"Well, I shall," said Bobby, and he wished it. "I wish I had a little aeroplane of my own that I could fly off in."

At once a most beautiful little aeroplane flew down from the air and landed beside Bobby. He was simply delighted. He got into it and grinned at Emma, who was very angry.

"You bad boy, to waste a wish on a thing like that!" she said, and she got up to go and shake him. She caught hold of his shoulders, and tried to pull him out of the aeroplane. "I wish you were

miles away!" she shouted. "You're a horrid brother to have!"

The aeroplane's engine started up, and the propeller began to whirl round. Emma's wish was coming true! Bobby was going to fly off miles away!

Bobby dragged Emma in beside him as the aeroplane flew off. "You horrid girl!" he said. "That's the second wish gone. Now goodness knows where we shall land."

They flew in the air for a long way and then the aeroplane landed on a little island. The sea splashed all round it, and except for a few strange trees and sea-birds there was nothing to be seen.

"Now see what you've done!" said Bobby. "Made us come here!" He got out of the aeroplane and walked round the little island. He came back looking gloomy. "We can't stay here. There is nothing to eat. We should starve. We must go back home."

"How?" said Emma.

"In the aeroplane," said Bobby. "Come on, get in. We'll fly back, and then we'll

be very, very careful about what we wish for our last wish."

They got into the aeroplane – but it didn't fly off. It just stood there, its engine silent and its propeller still.

"I'm afraid we'll have to use our last wish to get back home," said Bobby, sadly. "How we have wasted them! Aeroplane, I wish you would take us back home."

The aeroplane flew up into the air and soon the children were back in the meadow again. They got out and looked at the nice little plane.

"Well, anyway, we've still got this

aeroplane," said Bobby. But even as he spoke the little pixie ran up, jumped into the plane, set the engine going, and flew off.

"What did I tell you?" shouted the pixie, leaning out of the aeroplane. "I said that three wishes would be wasted on children like you and so they were! People who quarrel always do stupid things – what silly children you are!"

Bobby and Emma looked after the little aeroplane as it flew above the trees. They were very sad.

"If we hadn't quarrelled, we'd have been able to talk over what we really wanted," said Emma. "We could have wished for some lovely things."

"Well, we will next time," said Bobby.

But there won't be a next time. Things like that don't happen twice!

Mr Twinks
Hurries Up!

Mr Twinks sat on the chair in his little office, fanning himself. He really felt quite tired out with all his hurrying and the bell-ringing.

Now Mr Twinks was a dawdler and he was always late for everything, so his wife asked Lucy Little for a magic bell which she hung on one of the buttons at the back of his trousers. It was an invisible bell, so Twinks didn't know it was there, of course. It rang every time he dawdled, and gave him a terrible shock.

"I'll just have a little rest," thought Twinks. But the bell didn't think so. No – it set up its loud ringing once again. *R-r-r-r-ring!* it went. *R-r-r-r-ring!*

Twinks jumped dreadfully. Where

could that bell be? It was somewhere behind him, he was sure! But no matter how quickly he turned round, he could never see a bell anywhere.

Jingle-jangle-jang! went the bell. Then it changed its sound again and went *Ding-a-ding-a-ding!*

Everyone came rushing into Mr Twinks's office. "Did you ring, sir?" cried one man.

"Yes, sir; did you ring, sir?" cried the office boy.

"No, I didn't," said Twinks crossly. "Go back to your work. Some bell must have been rung by mistake." He began to tidy his desk and the bell stopped ringing. Twinks sat down to look through his morning letters. They were dull. After a bit he yawned and thought he would go out and get a morning cup of coffee.

But no sooner had he made up his mind to do that instead of getting on with his work, than the bell began to ring again – goodness, it sounded as loud as the fire-bell!

All the shop assistants came tearing

in again at once, gaping in surprise at the loud bell.

"Did you ring, sir?"

"You rang, sir?"

"Yes, sir, yes, sir?"

"Go out, go out!" shouted Mr Twinks in a rage. "No, I didn't ring. I don't know what's ringing. I wish it would stop!"

Everyone went out again, alarmed and astonished. Whatever was that bell then, if it wasn't Mr Twinks ringing?

Twinks put on his hat and went out to

escape the bell. But it rang loudly behind him all the way to the coffee-shop, and when he got there Mr Twinks felt he really couldn't go into the shop. He began to feel that the bell had something to do with himself. What would people in the shop say if the bell rang all the time?

So Twinks turned back and ran, yes *ran*, back to the bookshop where he worked! And, of course, the bell stopped ringing at once. That seemed rather strange to Twinks. He began to think about it.

"That bell seems to ring when I'm being slow or lazy – and stops when I'm hurrying or working," he thought. "It's funny – very funny."

He went into his office. He picked up his letters and began to answer them. He worked quite hard until it was nearly lunch-time. All his assistants left to go to their lunch and it was time for Twinks to go too. He leaned back in his chair. He was tired. He wouldn't hurry – his lunch could wait!

But – *R-r-r-rring! Ding-a-ding-a-ding!*

The noise made Twinks leap out of his chair as if he had been shot.

"Be quiet!" he said to the bell. "Be quiet, can't you? I'm going – I'm going as fast as I can!"

Ding! said the bell and stopped ringing, for Twinks was now hurrying out of the shop as fast as he could go. He almost ran home – and for the first time in his life was in time for lunch! Mrs Twinks was surprised and pleased.

"That bell has been worrying me a lot this morning," said Twinks. "I've discovered that it rings whenever it thinks I'm being slow – and it stops when I hurry."

"Very peculiar, dear," said Mrs Twinks, handing her husband a plate of hot stew.

"But if that bell thinks it's going to treat me like that, it's mistaken!" said Twinks fiercely. "Ringing at me like that! Deafening me! Making people turn round and stare – making people rush into my office and shout 'Did you ring, sir? – did you ring, sir?' I won't have it!"

"I should think not, Twinky!" said Mrs Twinks, giggling a little to herself, as she thought of all that happened.

Twinks sat down after lunch to look at the newspaper. He read and then he shut his eyes and fell asleep. Mrs Twinks didn't wake him. She knew that the magic bell would. And it did!

This time it decided to make a noise like a church bell. So it began:

Dong! Dong! Dong! Dong!

Twinks awoke with a start and leaped out of his chair. "Church time!" he cried. "We shall be late for church!"

Then he remembered that it was

Tuesday and he looked puzzled. "Oh! It's that tiresome bell again! If only I could find it I'd smash it to bits!"

The bell rang loudly like a telephone – *R-r-ring-r-r-ring!* It sounded just as if it were laughing at poor Twinks.

Twinks crammed his hat on his head and went out to his shop. He was in good time for once, and discovered that not one of his assistants was there. It was two o'clock, and the shop was supposed to be open then, but it was still shut and no one could get in to buy any books, however much they wanted to. Twinks was simply furious.

When at last the three assistants appeared, he was very angry with them. "How long has this lateness been going on?" he cried.

"Just as long as you yourself have been late," said the office-boy, cheekily.

"Now, a little more rudeness from you and you'll leave at once!" shouted Mr Twinks, glaring. All the same, it made him think a little. After all, how could he expect his helpers to be early if he was always late himself. It was a shocking example for him to set. Dear, dear! This really wouldn't do!

Twinks worked hard for the rest of the day. He was home in good time for dinner. The bell didn't ring once and Twinks was glad. But he spoiled everything by not wanting to go to bed. He sat yawning by the fire, while poor Mrs Twinks tried to make him go upstairs.

"All right, all right, there's no hurry," said Twinks – and then he jumped so much that he trod on the cat's tail and it leaped across the hearth-rug and tripped

up poor Mrs Twinks! The bell began to ring again!

This time it was like a fire-bell, and what a noise it made. "It'll wake all the neighbours!" cried Mrs Twinks. "Oh dear, oh dear!"

Twinks ran across the room in a hurry. He rushed upstairs and began to undress. The bell stopped ringing at once. Twinks did hope that the fire brigade wouldn't turn out. It was simply dreadful having a bell like that which went off at any time!

Mrs Twinks waited till Mr Twinks was in bed, and then she felt about for the magic bell. She found it, still hanging from one of the buttons at the back of his trousers. She took it off. She was sorry for Twinks and thought he had had enough of the bell. Poor Twinks.

Twinks was up early in the morning. He hurried through his breakfast. He was early at the shop – and who should be there but old Mr Booky, ready to give Twinks a good scolding! But he was so early that Mr Booky was pleased.

"Dear, dear – how punctual you are!" he said to Twinks. "I was going to tell you that you couldn't have your job any longer, because you are always so late – but if you have turned over a new leaf, and are going to be early and hard-working, I will let you keep your job!"

"Oh, Mr Booky, I want to keep my work!" cried Twinks in alarm, glad he was early for once. "Yes, yes – I have turned over a new leaf – lots of new leaves! I'm always going to be early and quick and hard-working in future, really I am!"

And to himself he said, "And I just won't have that tiresome bell ringing at me any more!"

He didn't know the bell was gone. He quite thought it was somewhere about still. And he was so anxious that it shouldn't ring that he hurried and scurried all day long, and really felt very busy and happy.

The bell didn't ring, of course. Mrs Twinks had taken it back to Lucy Little – and how Lucy laughed when she heard

what had happened! "I expect he's learned his lesson by now," she said. "It doesn't usually take more than a day, you know. I'm glad you brought the bell back, my dear. A mother has just come in to borrow it. She says she wants it for her child, who is so dawdly and lazy. So I can give it to her, can't I?"

Lucy Little gave the bell to the grateful mother and she hurried off with it – and some child is going to be very, very puzzled this week by a bell that rings behind him just when he is feeling dawdly. Let me know if it's you, won't you, because I would dearly like to borrow the bell for someone I know!

The Spell That Didn't Stop

Old Dame Quick-Eye put her head round the kitchen door and lazy little Yawner jumped up at once.

"What! Reading again in the middle of the morning before you've done your work!" scolded Dame Quick-Eye. "Do you want me to put a spell on you and make you grow two more arms and hands? Then you'd have to do twice as much work!"

"Oh no, no," cried Yawner, shutting his book and beginning to bustle round at once. "Don't do that."

"I have three friends coming to lunch," said Dame Quick-Eye. "There are all the potatoes and apples to peel and the cabbage to cut up. I shall be very angry if everything isn't ready in time."

Yawner was very frightened when Dame Quick-Eye was angry. As soon as she had gone he rushed into the kitchen.

"The potatoes! The potatoes! Where are they? And what did I do with those cabbages? Did I fetch them from the garden or didn't I? Where's the potato knife? Where is it?"

The potato knife was nowhere to be found. Yawner looked everywhere. "Oh dear, oh dear – the only sharp knife I have! I can't peel the potatoes with a blunt one. I'll never have time to do all this peeling!"

The front door slammed. Yawner saw Dame Quick-Eye going down the path. He stopped rushing about and sat down. He yawned widely. "Oh dear, what am I to do? I'd better get a spell from the old dame's room. A spell to peel potatoes and apples! She'll never know."

He tiptoed upstairs to the strange little room where Dame Quick-Eye did her magic and her spells. There they all were, in boxes and bottles on the shelf:

SPELL FOR MAKING THINGS BIG. SPELL

FOR MAKING THINGS SMALL. SPELL FOR
CURING A GREEDY PERSON. SPELL FOR
GROWING MORE ARMS AND HANDS. SPELL
TO CURE YAWNER OF BEING LAZY.

"Oh dear," said Yawner staring at the bottle with his name on the label. "I'd better not be lazy any more. Now – where's the spell to peel things quickly? Ah, here it is – good," he said at last, and picked up a box. In it was a green powder. Yawner hurried downstairs and took up an ordinary knife. He rubbed a little of the green powder on the blade.

"Now, peel!" he whispered. "Peel quickly, quickly. Don't stop!"

He rushed upstairs again and put the little box of powder back on the shelf, then down he went. Dame Quick-Eye would never know he had taken a bit of her peeling spell.

The spell was already working. The knife was hovering over the heap of potatoes, and one by one they rose up to be peeled, the peelings falling back on to the draining-board with a plop. "A very pleasant sight to see," thought Yawner, and he bustled about getting ready the things he needed to lay the table.

The knife peeled all the potatoes in about two minutes, then it started on

the apples. Soon long green parings were scattered all over the draining-board and a dozen apples lay clean and white nearby.

Yawner shot a glance at the busy knife. "Splendid, splendid! Take a rest, dear knife."

He rushed into the dining-room to lay the lunch. He rushed back into the kitchen to get the plates – and how he stared! The knife was peeling the cold chicken that Yawner had put ready for lunch. It was scraping off long bits of chicken, which fell to the floor and were being eaten by a most surprised and delighted cat.

"Hey!" cried Yawner and rushed at the knife. "Stop that! You've done your work!"

He tried to catch the knife but it flew to the dresser and peeled a long strip from that. Then it began to scrape the mantelpiece and big pieces of wood fell into the hearth.

Yawner began to feel frightened. What would Dame Quick-Eye say when she saw all this damage? He rushed at the knife again, but it flew up into the air, darted into the passage and disappeared.

"Well, good riddance to bad rubbish, I say," said Yawner loudly, and ran to put the potatoes on to boil. He heard Dame Quick-Eye come in with her friends and hurried himself even more. Lunch mustn't be late!

Then he heard such a to-do in the dining-room and rushed to see what the matter was. What a sight met his eyes!

The knife had peeled all the edges of the polished dining-room table. It had peeled every banana, orange, pear and apple in the dishes. It had peeled the backs of all the chairs, and even peeled the top off the clock.

"Look at this!" cried Dame Quick-Eye in a rage. "What's been happening? This knife is mad!"

"Bewitched, you mean," said one of her friends, looking at it closely. "I can see some green powder on the blade.

137

Someone's been rubbing it with your peeling spell."

"It's that wretched, tiresome, lazy little Yawner then!" cried Dame Quick-Eye. "And there he is – peeping in at the door. Wait till I catch you!"

Yawner didn't wait to hear more. He ran out into the garden. He kept his broomstick there, and he leaped on it at once.

"Off and away!" he shouted and up into the air rose the broomstick at once.

The broomstick soon became tired of going for miles and miles. It turned itself round and went back home again. It sailed down to the yard. Yawner leaped off and rushed to the coal-cellar. He went in and slammed the door. Then he sank down on the coal and cried. Why had he been lazy? Why had he ever stolen a spell? Wrong deeds never, never did any good at all.

Dame Quick-Eye looked in at the cellar window. She felt sorry for Yawner.

"Will you be lazy again?" she asked.

"No, Mam," wept Yawner.

"Will you ever steal my spells again?" she asked.

"No, Mam," said Yawner. "Never."

"Then come out and wash up the dirty plates and dishes," said Dame Quick-Eye, opening the door. "I've caught the knife and wiped the spell from it. You did a silly and dangerous thing."

"Yes, Mam," said Yawner mournfully, and went off to do the dishes.

Dame Quick-Eye hasn't had to use the special "Spell to cure Yawner of being lazy". In fact, she only has to mention spells to make Yawner work twice as hard as usual.

The Ship in
the Bottle

Uncle Tom had something very strange on his mantelpiece. When John and Robert went to stay with him it was always the very first thing they looked at.

It was a fully-rigged ship inside a bottle! The boys looked and looked at it. They simply couldn't make out how the ship got into the bottle.

"It nearly fills the bottle," said John, "and yet the neck of the bottle is so narrow that nobody, nobody could get the ship through it – so how did the ship get there?"

Uncle Tom didn't know either. "Must be magic!" he said. "I don't know how it's done. Your aunt bought it at a sale one day and there it's been ever since, sailing away on my mantelpiece, inside the bottle! It's a lovely thing, isn't it? Your aunt is very fond of it."

Aunt Julia came into the room. "Are you two boys staring at that ship again! I believe you like it better than anything in the house. I like it too – it's strange, isn't it? Goodness knows how the ship got into the bottle but there it sails, year in and year out."

"I guess it wishes it could sail just for once on real water," said Robert. "It's a proper little ship, Aunt Julia, and all the sail are exactly right, all fully-rigged and set correctly. It's a marvel, that ship!"

"Well, don't you mess about with it," said Uncle Tom. "I don't want the bottle broken – the ship would break then, too."

When Dick from over the road came to tea the boys showed the ship to him. Dick stared at it in surprise. "A ship inside a bottle! I've never seen that before. I say – it's strange isn't it? How did it get there? Nobody could get a ship as big as that through the neck of the bottle." He picked it up, and the two boys shouted at him at once.

"Don't touch it! Put it back!"

But Dick was obstinate. He held it in his hand and examined it closely. "All those sails full set," he said, "and the mast—"

"Put it back!" said John, fiercely, and he snatched at it. Dick held on, and swung himself round to get away from John's hand. He caught his foot in the hearth-rug and fell over.

Crash! The bottle fell to the floor and broke neatly in half. The little ship stayed

in one half, for it was stuck tightly there – but the top of its main-mast was broken off.

The three boys stared down in dismay. "You idiot!" said John, angrily. "Look what you've done!"

"If you hadn't grabbed at me it wouldn't have happened," said Dick, sulkily. "It's all your fault."

"It isn't! It's your fault for taking the bottle off the mantelpiece in the first place," said John, fiercely. "My uncle will be furious. You can jolly well go and own up."

"Well, I'm not going to," said Dick, stalking out of the room. "It *wasn't* my fault. Just like you to try to put the blame on someone else."

He went out of the house and ran across the road to his own home. Robert and John looked at each other. "Let's go and tell Uncle now," said Robert. "I bet Dick will get into a row."

"Well – that would be telling tales, and Uncle doesn't like that," said John. "Look, let's put the two halves together

and get some glue or something. Perhaps we can mend it so that nobody will notice."

"No. That's as bad as telling tales!" said Robert. "You know it is! Oh blow! It was such a lovely thing and now it's spoilt."

"Well – can we possibly get another bottle and put the ship into it somehow ourselves?" said John. "Let's try. Somebody once put it in, so perhaps we can."

"We could try that," said Robert. "Let's try at once. Uncle and Auntie are out. We might be able to do it before they get back. Then it won't be so bad having to own up."

They went to the cupboard where jars and bottles were kept. They took out an empty bottle very much the same as the broken one. Then, carrying the ship very carefully in one of the broken pieces, they went to their bedroom. John looked at the ship closely.

"Isn't it beautifully made?" he said. "I'm glad it wasn't badly broken – look, only the mast-tip has gone. Now, the first thing is to get it off this broken half. Look how someone has painted a bit of wood the colour of the sea for it to sail on, Robert."

They chipped the ship and the wooden waves carefully off the broken glass. Then they got the bottle they had found. But it was absolutely impossible to get the ship through the neck – it was far too tall, with its lovely masts and beautiful sails.

"No good!" said John, putting it down. "Quite, quite impossible. But how did anyone ever get it into a bottle? It simply must be magic."

"Hello!" said Aunt Julia, suddenly opening the door. "I wondered where you were. Oh – surely, surely you haven't taken that ship out of the bottle! However did it get broken?"

"Well, it fell on the floor," said John, going red. "And the bottle broke."

"I told you not to take it off the mantelpiece," said Aunt Julia, vexed. "I'm surprised at you. You know how fond of that ship Uncle and I are."

Robert longed to say it was Dick who had broken it, but John frowned at him. He did so hate telling tales. The boys at school hated a sneak but all the same it was very hard to take the blame for somebody else.

"It's no good trying to poke it into that bottle," said Aunt Julia, still very cross. "You'll only break the whole ship up. I really do feel annoyed with you. I only hope Uncle won't send you back home. You know what he thinks of disobedience!"

She went out of the room. The two boys felt alarmed. It would be dreadful to be sent back home in disgrace. But John soon cheered up.

"Aunt Julia wouldn't send us home. I know she wouldn't. She's cross now, but she's very kind really. I wish we could do something to make up for this – even though it isn't our fault."

"Let's tell Auntie it was Dick," said Robert. "Anyway, if Uncle says he's going to send us home, will you tell then?"

"Well, I might then," said John. "Look,

I'll tell you what we'll do. I'll get the mower and mow the grass for Uncle before he comes home and you go and clean Aunt Julia's garden tools. That'll be just a little something to make up for the ship."

So when Aunt Julia looked out of the window, there was John mowing the grass, and Robert busily cleaning her tools. She couldn't help smiling.

"Trying to show they're sorry, I suppose!" she said. "Well, that's something! Naughty little boys!"

The ship was put into a cupboard because Auntie said it would get so dusty now that it was no longer in a bottle. The boys were sad. "Now nobody will see it again," said John, "except us if we go and peep at it. Blow Dick!"

Uncle had been cross, but not quite so cross as he might have been if his lawn hadn't been so beautifully cut! Nothing more was said about the ship. Auntie threw away the broken halves of the bottle, and was her own kind self again.

Two days later Dick came creeping in at the garden door to find John and Robert. He knew that their Uncle and Aunt were out. He looked rather shamefaced, and kept his head down when he spoke to them.

"I say – I saw your aunt and uncle go out. Are they very cross with me? Are they going to tell my dad? What did they say when you told them I'd broken the bottle?"

"We didn't tell them," said John. "We aren't sneaks. If you didn't own up, we weren't going to tell tales. We got into trouble for it, instead of you. You're mean. Aunt Julia said Uncle might send us home in disgrace."

Dick raised his head in surprise at all this. "What! Didn't you tell them I broke the bottle?" he said. "Gosh, I've been worrying no end about it – that lovely ship – and being afraid your uncle would come over to my dad about it. I knew I'd get into trouble if he did. I didn't sleep at all the night before last."

"Serves you right," said Robert,

hardheartedly. "I wanted to tell. You're a coward not to own up! We don't want to play with you any more. Go on home."

Dick went very red. He didn't like being spoken to like that. He looked at the mantelpiece. "Where's the ship?" he said.

"In that cupboard, where nobody ever sees it," said John. "The broken bottle has been thrown away. Don't come over here again, Dick. We don't want you."

Dick went, looking miserable. He sat and thought hard in a corner of his garden at home. He must own up! It was so decent of John and Robert not to sneak. What a pity he had broken that bottle with the ship inside.

He suddenly thought of something. Down at the jetty by the shore was an old sailor called Salty, who was very clever with his hands. He could mend any boat in the bay, he could make nets of all kinds, and his great thick fingers could even work with shells and seaweed, and make quaint treasures to sell to visitors. Would he know anything about ships in

bottles? Perhaps he even had one to sell!

Dick took down his piggy-bank from the mantelpiece. It was a china pig with a slit in his back, and a little door in his tummy that could be unlocked. Dick didn't know how much a ship in a bottle was, but he was quite prepared to pay out every penny he had if he could get one. He thought that John and Robert had behaved in a surprisingly generous way, and he felt very small and mean. He would go on feeling like that till he somehow put things right!

He had ten pounds in the pig. It seemed a large sum to Dick. Surely that would buy a new ship in a bottle?

He went to find Salty. There he was, sitting on an upturned boat, busy at something. Dick went up to him.

"Salty, you haven't got a ship in a bottle to sell, have you?" he asked.

"No. It's a long time since I made one of those," said Salty. "Tricky things they are. Very tricky. Getting them into the bottle is a fiddly job!"

"Oh – do you know how to do that?" said Dick, suddenly excited. He told Salty all about the broken bottle and the beautiful little ship.

"Salty – if I bring you the ship, could you possibly get it into the bottle?" he asked, eagerly. "Could you?"

"Oh, ay. I couldn't make the ship nowadays but I know how to get one into a bottle," said Salty. "You bring it along and I'll do it for you."

"Will you do it for ten pounds?" asked Dick. "That's all I've got."

"Well, seeing that it was your fault the bottle got broken, you ought to pay something for it," said Salty. "You give me half the money. That'll be all right."

"Oh, thank you!" said Dick joyfully, and ran off to find John and Robert and tell them the news.

They could hardly believe their ears. "What! Salty knows how to get the ship into the bottle?" said John. "How does he do it?"

"I didn't ask him. We could watch

him," said Dick. "Where's the ship? Come on, let's take it and see if Salty really can do it!"

They took the little ship from the cupboard and raced down to Salty with it. He grinned at them, and took the ship in his great brown hand.

"Ah – she's a tidy little ship," he said. "A little beauty. Look, I've got a bottle that will fit her well. Nice and clean it is, too."

The boys stayed the whole morning with him, watching him. First he mended the top of the broken mast very cleverly indeed. Then he touched up the ship here and there with paint, so that she gleamed fresh and new.

Then he began to jiggle with the masts a little. "What are you doing?" said John. "Don't break them, for goodness sake!"

Salty laughed – and at that moment one of the masts fell down flat on the ship's deck, taking its sails with it. The boys groaned.

"Now you've broken that mast," said John.

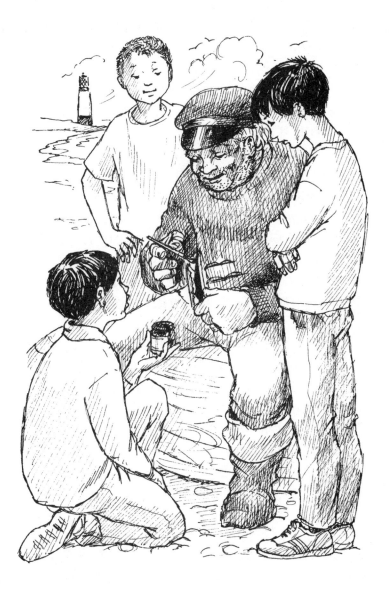

"Nay – I haven't," said Salty, with a grin. Just then down went the second mast and the rest of the sails lay flat too!

"They're not broken – they're hinged at the bottom," said Salty. "Look close and you'll see. That's the secret of getting the ship into the bottle. Now watch!"

The ship's hull was set fast in the painted wooden strip of sea. Mast and sails lay flat. Salty picked up the ship and the bottle. He held the ship near the bottle-neck and twinkled at the boys. "See how easily she'll go in now the masts and sails are flat on the hull? Easy!"

"Oh, yes! She's small enough now to slip inside!" cried Dick. "I never thought of that! But Salty – how will you get the masts and sails upright again, once the hull is in the bottle?"

"Ah now, you watch and see," said Salty, putting down the bottle. The three boys bent their head over his deft fingers as he worked on the masts with tiny threads. He fastened a thread to each mast with a slip-knot.

"Now, watch again," he said, and slid the hull of the ship into the bottle-neck. It slid right through it into the main part of the bottle, where Salty had smeared some glue with a brush. It stuck there standing in the correct position. The threads from the fallen masts hung out of the neck of the bottle.

Salty pulled one carefully. The mast rose upright in the bottle and took the sails with it. He pulled the other thread and the second mast rose too. Now the little ship was in full sail!

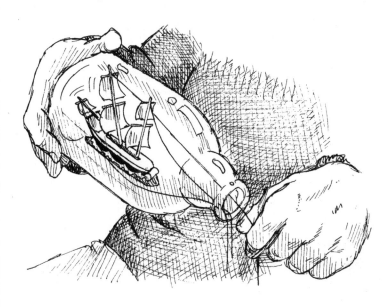

Salty drew the threads out and threw them away. He sealed up the bottle and gave it to Dick.

"There you are!" he said. "That's how all ships are put into bottles. No magic about it – just a little ingenuity and careful handling. Take care of it this time, and don't break the bottle!"

"Oh! That was well worth the money," said Dick, delighted, and he took the bottle from Salty. "Thank you. Come on, you others. I'm going to take it to your uncle and own up!"

Uncle Tom was amazed to see Dick holding the ship, safely in a bottle again. He listened gravely to what the boy said.

"I broke the bottle, and I wouldn't own up. And the others didn't tell tales on me so you didn't know. I'm sorry, Mr Gray. I've got the ship mended again. Salty did it!"

"Splendid!" said Uncle Tom and patted Dick on the shoulder. "I'm glad you owned up. It's cowardly not to. John and Robert, I'm sorry I was cross with you, but I didn't know. And to think you

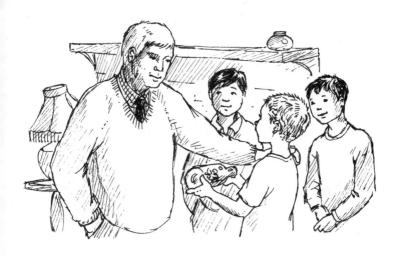

mowed the grass and cleaned your aunt's tools too, so cheerfully!"

"Tom! They deserve a reward!" said Aunt Hilda, suddenly. "Give them the ship! It would have been no use to us unmended and now it's so beautiful again, I think they should have it."

So John and Robert have it for their own now, and it's on their mantelpiece at home. Did you know how a ship got into a bottle? I didn't – but I'm glad Salty told us all about it!

The Boy Who Broke His Promises

Andrew was the boy who broke his promises. He was such a nice boy to look at, his eyes were so bright and his smile so merry – and yet nobody could trust him!

"I'll do my homework as soon as I finish my tea," he promised his mother each day. But after tea he ran off to play, and forgot all about his homework.

"I'll never bite my nails again!" he promised his teacher, when she said how dreadful his bitten nails were. But the very next minute his fingers were in his mouth, and he was nibbling at his poor, ugly nails!

"I'll put away my toys and not leave one out," he told his aunt when she came to look after him one day. But he forgot, and his promise was broken.

"Andrew, promises are made to be kept and not to be broken," his mother said. "What is the use of making promises you never keep? People will not trust you."

"Oh, I always mean to keep my promises," said Andrew. "But I forget."

His mother was worried. She didn't want him to grow up into somebody that could not be trusted to keep his word. So she told Andrew's old Great-Aunt May, who nodded her snow-white head.

"Send him to me for a few days," she said. "I'll cure him for you!"

So Andrew's bag was packed and he set off in the bus to Great-Aunt May. He

had never been to her house before, but he knew her very well, because she often came to his mother's house, and she always brought him a present.

Great-Aunt May was pleased to see him. She took him upstairs to his little bedroom. It was very cosy.

"I hope you'll try and keep your room tidy for me," she said.

"Oh yes, I promise it will always be as neat as can be," said Andrew. But as soon as Great-Aunt had gone out of the room he tipped his bag up, and out fell everything at once! And there Andrew left them. He just simply couldn't be trusted to keep his word about anything!

He went downstairs. "What's for tea, Great-Aunt?" he said.

"Well, how would you like buns with jam and cream inside, and chocolate cake with walnuts on top?" asked Great-Aunt.

"Oooh!" said Andrew. "Super!"

"Very well, I'll get them," said Great-Aunt. So Andrew longed and longed for teatime, and rushed into the dining-room when Great-Aunt May called him.

But do you know, there was only bread-and-butter and plain biscuits on the table! No buns – and no cake at all.

"Oh, Great-Aunt! Where are the jammy buns with cream, and the chocolate cake with walnuts that you promised?" asked Andrew.

"Dear me, I quite forgot about them," said Great-Aunt May.

"But, Great-Aunt, you promised, and promises shouldn't be broken," said Andrew, almost crying.

"That's so," said the old lady. "But still, you promised to keep your room neat for me, Andrew, and it is in a dreadful mess. So as you broke your promise, perhaps you won't mind me breaking mine. Now, eat up your bread-and-butter."

"Great-Aunt, may I stay up till eight o'clock tonight?" said Andrew, who usually went to bed at seven.

"Yes, if you like," promised Great-Aunt. "It will be a treat for you! Get my scissors after tea, Andrew, and go and snip all the dead flowers off in the front garden for me, will you? There are such a lot, and I shall be too busy to do them today."

"Yes, I will, Great-Aunt," promised Andrew. But after tea he wandered down to the field at the bottom of the garden, and played at cowboys and Indians there, crawling in and out of the hedge, and yelling loudly whenever he saw the dog next door. The dog was supposed to be an enemy cowboy.

"Oh, bother!" he said to himself, when he remembered that he had said he would snip off the dead flowers for Great-

Aunt May. "It's a nuisance to stop my play. I'll do Great-Aunt's job tomorrow."

Suddenly the bell rang to call him indoors. Andrew went. Great-Aunt was upstairs.

"Bedtime!" she called. "Hurry up, because I have to go out soon and I want you in bed first."

"But, Great-Aunt, you promised I could stay up till eight o'clock!" said Andrew. "It's only seven!"

"Oh, well, I've changed my mind," said Great-Aunt. "And you changed yours about snipping off the dead flowers for me, so that makes us even! You broke your promise and I broke mine! Hurry now, and don't look so miserable. I'll give you a sweet orange when you're in bed. Remember to wash yourself well, won't you? I have run the water in the bath."

"Yes, Great-Aunt," said Andrew gloomily, and he got undressed. He got into the nice hot bath but he didn't bother about washing, and suddenly he heard his Great-Aunt's voice from downstairs.

"Are you in bed yet?"

"Nearly!" shouted Andrew, jumping out of the bath and dragging on his pyjamas without drying himself! He brushed his hair and jumped into bed.

His great-aunt came into the room.

"Have you brought my nice juicy orange that you promised me?" asked Andrew.

"Oh, bother! No, I haven't!" said Great-Aunt May. "Never mind, you can have it tomorrow."

"But you promised I could have it now!" said Andrew, thinking that really Great-Aunt couldn't be trusted at all!

"Well, you promised to wash yourself well in the bath, and as far as I can see, your face is still as dirty as when I left you, and your hands are quite black," said Great-Aunt. "I expect if I looked at your knees they would be just as bad. So you can't blame me if I don't keep my promises, Andrew. Perhaps I should be a bit more particular about it if you kept yours."

The next day was just as bad. Great-Aunt promised all sorts of wonderful things, and Andrew felt most excited when he heard them.

"There's a circus coming this afternoon," said his great-aunt. "We might go to see it. I think it is in the field nearby. Oh, and what would you like for lunch? Would you like an ice-cream pudding?"

"Oh yes!" said Andrew, who liked ice cream better than anything else. "And Great-Aunt, would you get out that lovely bow and arrows that belonged to Great-Uncle years ago? I'd love to play with the bow."

"Yes, I'll get it out this morning," said Great-Aunt May. "That's a promise!"

Well, it may have been a promise, but Great-Aunt May didn't keep it! When

Andrew went to ask for the bow and arrows, she was busy cooking in the kitchen.

"Go away, dear, I'm busy!" she said. "I haven't bothered about the bow this morning. I don't know where it is."

"But Great-Aunt, you did promise!" cried Andrew.

"And who promised to make his bed this morning and didn't?" said Great-Aunt. "And who promised to fetch me the eggs from the hen-house and didn't? And who promised to fill the bird-bath with water and didn't?"

Andrew went red. Had he really made all those promises and broken them? Well, then, he really couldn't blame Great-Aunt for doing as he did. He went out without another word.

At lunch-time he ate his meat and potatoes and gravy eagerly, hoping that the ice-cream pudding would be very large indeed. But do you know, there was only a small rice pudding and nothing else!

"Great-Aunt! You've broken your promise again!" cried Andrew. "You said we'd have ice-cream pudding!"

"Did I really?" said Great-Aunt. "Oh, well, I forgot. I suppose you forgot to

change your shoes when you came in, Andrew. You promised you would change them, but I see there is mud on the carpet. And I believe you said you would wash your hands. Well, well – you forgot, and I forgot. So we won't blame each other, will we?"

Andrew went red. He ate his rice pudding without a word. All the time he ate it he was thinking about the circus. Would Great-Aunt keep her promise about that? He hardly dared to ask her. If only, only she would!

Well she didn't! When Andrew went to remind her at half past two, she was in her bedroom, having a rest on her bed. She was quite cross at being disturbed.

"Circus! Who said anything about a circus?" she cried. "I may have promised to take you this morning but I've changed my mind this afternoon. I'm tired and I want a rest. Go away."

"But Great-Aunt, you promised, you really did!" said Andrew, and burst into tears.

"Come here, Andrew," said Great-Aunt

May in a funny sort of voice. So Andrew went and stood beside her.

"Andrew, do you like me when I break my promises?" said Great-Aunt May. "Do you trust me any more?"

"No," said Andrew. "I don't feel as if I do trust you, Great-Aunt. And I don't like you at all when you break your word. It makes me feel so disappointed and angry."

"Well, you know, Andrew, I've just been doing it to show you what people think of you when you keep promising things and forgetting them," said Great-Aunt. "It's horrid, isn't it? It's quite enough to make people cry and feel cross. That is how you make people feel, too, when you break your promises, Andrew."

"Great-Aunt, I will really try now to keep my promises – all of them," promised Andrew. "I didn't know how horrid I made people feel when I broke them. I won't do it again."

"Well, you'll find it difficult at first," said Great-Aunt. "But you must keep on trying. Now, will you promise me to weed that untidy bit of garden this afternoon, and to wash your hands for tea, and change your muddy shoes?"

"Yes, Great-Aunt," said Andrew.

"And I will promise you jammy, creamy buns for tea again, and chocolate cake with walnuts, and the circus tonight!" said Great-Aunt. "We will see how we can manage to keep our promises!"

Well, Andrew weeded the garden, and

washed his hands, and changed his shoes – and sure enough there were jammy, creamy buns for tea, and chocolate cake, and they went to the circus that night!

Andrew kept his promises next day too, and there was ice-cream pudding for lunch, and he was allowed to play with the wonderful bow and arrows all morning! He went to bed at eight o'clock for a treat, and had a juicy orange.

He was quite sorry to go home. But, dear me, how surprised his mother was to find Andrew so changed! If he said he would do a thing, he did it. If he promised he wouldn't, he didn't.

"Why, Andrew, I really believe you are to be trusted after all!" said his mother. And so he was. But he never told her how Great-Aunt May had cured him. He was rather ashamed of that!

I am sure you keep your promises – but if you know anyone who doesn't, send them along to Great-Aunt May. She'll soon cure them!

The
Enchanted Pencil

Nobody liked Nippy very much. He was a small soft-footed goblin, and you couldn't leave anything about when he was near, in case he slipped away with it.

"Now where's my bag of groceries gone?" Dame Toddle would say. "I just put it down on that chair for a moment – and then I look round and it's gone!"

So it had – and Nippy had gone with it. Nothing was safe near him, not even a box of matches. Into Nippy's pocket it would go. He had gone off with Mr Shabby's library book, Mother Rose's gloves, and a bag of sweets belonging to Tiny, the pixie. Nobody ever saw him take anything – but everybody knew!

"I can't go after him unless I have proof," said Mr Plod the policeman.

"Can't accuse anyone without proof, you know. All I can say is be careful, all of you, and don't leave your things about!"

"We don't leave them about – we only put them down for a moment," said Dame Toddle. "I put my bag of groceries down to get out my purse, that's all, and lo and behold, it disappears in an instant!"

"We'll have to chain all our belongings to us," said Mother Rose, gloomily. "What he wants with my gloves I don't know. They wouldn't fit his big, bony hands."

When Dame Sharp-Eye came to stay with Mother Rose, she heard all about Nippy. "And really I don't know what we can do about him," said Mother Rose. "He's quite impossible."

"Oh, I think I can manage to deal with him for you," said Dame Sharp-Eye. "You leave it to me."

"Can you really?" said Mother Rose. "That would be marvellous."

Dame Sharp-Eye went and rummaged in her bag upstairs. She took out a little narrow box, rather long. In it was a pencil – a most peculiar one!

It was green and gold, and had a curious sharp point at the bottom of it, like the sting of an insect. When it wrote the writing was beautiful – sharp, strong and black. It was a very smart pencil indeed.

"Ah, there you are, my little magic pencil," said Dame Sharp-Eye, pleased. "I'm glad I brought you with me. Now see you work your magic properly when you leave me."

The pencil stood up by itself, waggled a bit and then dropped down again.

"You've plenty of magic still in you, although you're so old," said Dame Sharp-Eye. "Now, into my handbag you go – and keep quiet while you're there."

She went down to Mother Rose. "I've found what I wanted," she said. "Tomorrow morning we will go shopping together, and we will go somewhere that Nippy is sure to be. We shall see some fun in a short while!"

So the next day out they went with their shopping bags. They went to the baker's. Nippy wasn't there. They went to the butcher's and then to the grocer's. Ah – there he was, collecting his groceries.

Dame Sharp-Eye looked at him. What a mean, shifty little goblin!

Yes, he needed a lesson all right. She took out her shopping list and her strange green and gold pencil. She put the pencil down on the counter.

Nippy saw it at once. His eyes gleamed. What a pencil! He could sell that for a lot of money to Sly-One the enchanter.

Dame Sharp-Eye bought a great many

things. Then she took up her pencil.
"Pencil, add up my bill," she said, and
hey presto, that pencil ran itself down
the bill and wrote down a sum of money
at the bottom.

Nippy's eyes nearly fell out of his head.
Good gracious! It wasn't only an
unusually beautiful pencil, but a magic
one, too. He really must get hold of it.

Dame Sharp-Eye put the pencil down
on the counter again and turned her back
on it to look at some plums in a box

nearby. In a flash Nippy's long arm reached out and snapped up the pencil. It went into his pocket at once, and he was out of the door before Dame Sharp-Eye had turned round.

But her sharp eye had seen everything all right! There was a little mirror in the shop, and although she had her back to the counter, she had seen Nippy snatch up the pencil and run off with it. She smiled at Mother Rose.

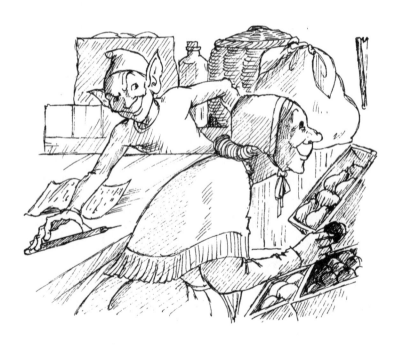

"He's taken it," she said. "Now there'll be some fun!"

Well, before Nippy had gone far he felt something pricking him. What could it be? He put his hand into his pocket to see if he had a pin there, and he felt a sharp prick in his hand. Goodness – had he got a bee in his pocket or something?

He didn't know it was the sharp point on the end of the pencil! He got a few more pricks before he reached home and couldn't think what they were.

He took the pencil out and looked at it gleefully. "My word! You'll be worth a lot of money!" he said. "This is a bit of luck! To think you can add up sums too. You can do all my bills for me."

The pencil wriggled in his hand and gave him a dig with its sharp end. Nippy dropped it at once. "Ooooh – so it was you that kept pricking me! You horrid thing! I'll take you to the enchanter Sly-One at once and get rid of you!"

But that pencil hopped off the table and took itself to the bare wall. It scribbled something there in large writing: *No, you won't! I'm staying here!*

Nippy stared at the writing in astonishment. What a very, very magic pencil this was!

"It's no good your being rude to me," he said to the pencil. "You're going to be sold to Sly-One the enchanter, and I'm taking you now!"

He made a dart at the pencil and it jabbed its sharp end into his hand again. Nippy howled. "Oh, you mean thing! You've got a sting!"

The pencil scribbled on the wall! *I only sting bad people. That's why I sting you!*

"Now you stop writing rude things about me," said Nippy angrily. "Suppose someone comes in and sees all that?"

He took a cloth and began to wipe off what the pencil had written. He went to the kitchen to rinse out the cloth. When he came back he stared at the wall in horror. The pencil had been doing a bit of writing again!

Nippy has got Mother Rose's best gloves in his top drawer. Isn't he a thief? the pencil had written. Nippy went pale.

Nippy has got Mother Rose's best gloves in his top drawer. Isn't he a thief?

Good gracious! Had the pencil been looking into his drawers? There were a lot of things there that Nippy didn't want anyone to see.

He grabbed at the pencil again and caught it. The pencil stung him hard and he dropped it with a yell. "I'll throw you in the fire next time I get you!" he shouted. The pencil at once went to write on the wall again.

Nippy is so afraid of me that he says he will throw me in the fire.

Rat-a-tat-tat! That was a knock at the door. Nippy stared in despair at the wall. Goodness, he couldn't possibly ask anyone in with that scribbling on the wall. He rushed to get a wet cloth again. Soon he had the writing washed away, and he went to open the door.

"Goodness – you've been long enough opening the door!" said little Nosy-One, the imp. "What's up?"

"Nothing," said Nippy. "What do you want? Come to pay me my bill?"

"No," said Nosy-One. "I've come to say I can't. You'll have to give me another week."

"I can't possibly," said Nippy. "I've no money at all, and I've my own bills to pay."

Nosy-One suddenly stared at the wall behind Nippy's head. Nippy felt most uncomfortable. Was that pencil writing anything else?

It was. It had written:

Nippy's got plenty of money in his left-hand drawer, and he's got a watch belonging to Father Timmy in the right-hand one. Shame on you, nasty Nippy!

"Oooh – is that a magic pencil?" said Nosy-One, in amazement. "Isn't it rude? Does it keep writing things like that about you? Have you really got Father Timmy's watch? Oooh, I'm glad I haven't got a pencil like that!"

And out he ran to tell Father Timmy that Nippy had got his watch, and to

spread the news that there was a very rude magic pencil at work in Nippy's house.

Father Timmy was soon round there. The wall had again been washed clean, but the pencil was hovering about, ready to begin its scribbling at any minute. Nippy had tried swatting at it with the fly-swatter, but the pencil was really very good at dodging.

"Have you got my watch, Nippy?" demanded Father Timmy sternly.

"No," said Nippy.

The pencil began writing in such a hurry that the words went all crooked:

Ooh! He's a storyteller as well as a thief! Look in the right-hand top drawer.

Father Timmy pushed Nippy aside and looked in the drawer. There was his watch. He looked sternly at the goblin.

"I'm going to Mr Plod about this."

Good! wrote the pencil. *Fetch Mr Plod!*

Father Timmy went out, frowning. Nippy stood glaring at the pencil. "Look here," he said, "will you please go away, back to your mistress, Dame Sharp-Eye?"

No, wrote the pencil. *I'm staying here for the rest of my life. It's a nice cottage – just what my mistress would like, too.*

"Well, either you go or I go," said Nippy, and he hit out at the pencil again. It stung him and then wrote quickly:

Well, I'm staying. Goodbye!

And goodbye it was, because Nippy didn't dare to stay with that enchanted pencil, and neither did he want to meet Mr Plod if he came back with Father Timmy. So he packed his bag and caught the very next bus out of the village.

"Where's Nippy?" said Mr Plod, when he came along with Father Timmy and Dame Sharp-Eye, who was expecting something of the sort.

Gone for good! wrote the pencil.

"Splendid," said Mr Plod. "It will be a good riddance to bad rubbish. Well, I'll search the house and see what stolen goods there are. Then we'll sell the furniture and give the money to the many people Nippy has robbed. But what shall we do with the house?"

"It's just what I want," said Dame Sharp-Eye at once. "I came to stay with

Mother Rose to look for a house here, Mr Plod. I want to live in this nice village. I'll have the house."

"We shall be delighted to have the owner of this remarkable pencil living in our village," said Father Timmy. "Do you agree, Mr Plod?"

"I certainly do," said the policeman. "I'm very, very grateful to you, Dame Sharp-Eye, for getting rid of that tiresome little nuisance. You shall certainly have this cottage as soon as ever it's ready."

The pencil scribbled quickly on the wall. *Hurrah!* it wrote. *Three cheers! I like this place.*

Dame Sharp-Eye laughed. "Well, pencil, you won't be allowed to write on the walls once I'm living here. You'll have to behave yourself."

And the pencil wrote, *I will!*